"You've got to stop sending me flowers, Sam."

Rachel had propped one hand on her hip, no doubt thinking that it made her look stern and no-nonsense. In truth, Sam admitted, it only made him think that she had a deliciously curved hip. He raised one brow and grinned. "You don't like daisies, Rachel?"

"You know darn well that I love daisies, Sam Grayson," she said. "The point is that you are clearly trying to bribe me."

"You like them, though, don't you? Even if they come from me?"

"I like them," she whispered, turning her head away.

She did. Sam knew that much. But he didn't know how to convince her to care for his children. She'd already said that it would be impossible for him to win this battle, so he should stop trying. He really should, but he knew he wouldn't.

Not yet, anyway.

Dear Reader,

What makes a man a Fabulous Father? For me, he's the man who married my single mother when she had three little kids (who all needed braces) and raised us as his own. And, to celebrate an upcoming anniversary of the Romance line's FABULOUS FATHERS series, I'd like to know *your* thoughts on what makes a man a Fabulous Father. Send me a brief (50 words) note with your name, city and state, giving me permission to publish all or portions of your note, and you just might see it printed on a special page.

Blessed with a baby—and a second chance at marriage—this month's FABULOUS FATHER also has to become a fabulous husband to his estranged wife in *Introducing Daddy* by Alaina Hawthorne.

"Will you marry me, in name only?" That's a woman's desperate question to the last of THE BEST MEN, Karen Rose Smith's miniseries, in *A Groom and a Promise.*

He drops her like a hot potato, then comes back with babies and wants her to be his nanny! Or so he says...in *Babies and a Blue-Eyed Man* by Myrna Mackenzie.

When a man has no memory and a woman needs an instant husband, she tells him a little white lie and presto! in *My Favorite Husband* by Sally Carleen.

She's a waitress who needs etiquette lessons in becoming a lady; he's a millionaire who likes her just the way she is in *Wife in Training* by Susan Meier.

Finally, Robin Wells is one of Silhouette's WOMEN TO WATCH—a new author debuting in the Romance line with *The Wedding Kiss.*

I hope you enjoy all our books this month—and every month!

Regards,

Melissa Senate,
Senior Editor

BABIES AND A BLUE-EYED MAN

Myrna Mackenzie

To Sue,
All the best!
Myrna Mackenzie

Silhouette®
ROMANCE™
Published by Silhouette Books
America's Publisher of Contemporary Romance

To my sister, Brenda—
Who led the way and helped inspire my own career change.
And to my brother, Dale—
Thanks for teaching me the value of a good chuckle.

SILHOUETTE BOOKS

ISBN 0-373-19182-0

BABIES AND A BLUE-EYED MAN

This edition published by arrangement with Harlequin Books S.A.

Printed in U.S.A.

Books by Myrna Mackenzie

Silhouette Romance

The Baby Wish #1046
The Daddy List #1090
Babies and a Blue-Eyed Man #1182

MYRNA MACKENZIE

has always been fascinated by the belief that within every man is a hero, and inside every woman lives a heroine. She loves to write about ordinary people making extraordinary dreams come true. A former teacher, Myrna lives in Illinois with her husband—who was her high school sweetheart—and her two sons. She believes in love, laughter, music, vacations to the mountains, watching the stars, avoiding the words *physical fitness* and letting the dust balls gather where they may.

The Language of Flowers

(Or, How To Win a Wife)

1. Start with red camellias, to assure her of her loveliness.
2. In case she's wondering about your motives, give her yellow daffodils and show her that chivalry is not dead.
3. Now that you have her interest, prove to her that your feelings are pure with a single white rose.
4. Snowdrops speak of hope, so if you're hankering for a future with her, better give her a bunch of these blossoms.
5. Here comes the big one: forget-me-nots. Since these flowers mean true love, you'd better get down on one knee when you hand them to her.
6. If everything works out okay, keep those flowers coming. After all, she'll need them when she takes that walk down the aisle....

Chapter One

It was four o'clock in the afternoon when Sam Grayson came home early and realized he needed to make a change in his life. His six-year-old daughter, Annie, was struggling with a needle and thread and a mangled bit of cloth. She had five bandages on her fingers and was in grave danger of stitching her nose to the fabric she was leaning over.

"Hi, Annie, love. What's that you're doing?"

She looked up at him with big blue eyes, blinking as she struggled to bring him into focus. Sam noticed her glasses lying on a nearby table. She was supposed to wear them all the time. "Daddy," she said, holding up the rumpled scrap of material. "*I* am sewing baby Zach's pajamas. He tored them."

Sam looked at the cloth. It was definitely ripped, but...

"Honey, Mrs. Nelson will do that. Shouldn't you be with your friends? I thought Lisa usually came over on Wednesdays."

"Oh, yes." Annie nodded. "She used to, but lately *I* have been too busy. The twins are babies and they need a mommy."

Sam's heart caught in his throat. How like Annie to note that her brother and sister needed a mother, when she had no mother herself. Or at least not one who was ever around.

Gently he removed the smudged bit of cloth from Annie's grasp and sank down on his knees next to her chair. He looked into her eyes that were so like his own. "Annie, sweetheart," he said, taking her hand and sandwiching it between his palms. "You're six years old, too young to be a mommy yet. You should be out in the sunshine, running, playing make-believe."

Annie's eyes had darkened at his first words, but she suddenly brightened and sat up straighter. "Oh, but I do play make-believe, Daddy. I tell stories to the twins every day after school. That's why Lisa doesn't come. She gets very grouchy when she has to wait for me to finish."

And why not? Sam thought, trying to find the words to turn his daughter into the bright, laughing child she'd once been. Why would Lisa want to wait around, when her friend had become a stranger? Silently he cursed himself. Things hadn't been right for Annie since Donna had walked out six months after the twins were born. They certainly hadn't been right since the divorce. But he hadn't known they'd been this wrong.

"What does Mrs. Nelson say about you taking care of the twins?" he asked, needing to know Annie's side of the story before he discussed this with his housekeeper.

"Oh, Mrs. Nelson." Annie shook her head. "She thinks I'm too little, just like you. But I'm not, Daddy. And Janey and Zach need me a lot. Not like that mean old Lisa Dobbins." Annie twisted her fingers and stared down at her lap.

Ah, now they were getting somewhere. Sam tucked one finger beneath his daughter's trembling chin. "Why is Lisa mean, Annie? I thought she was your best friend."

"No, no, she's not," Annie nearly shouted. "She said my mommy was bad and that Mommy left because she didn't love me. Lisa said *her* mommy loved her so much she would never leave. Not ever."

Long streaky tears traced their way down Annie's cheeks as she choked out the last words. Sam held out his arms, sitting back and pulling her onto his lap as he smoothed circles over her sharp little shoulder blades with his palm.

Dammit, how could Donna have done this? Hadn't she known how much her desertion would cost Annie? The note she'd pinned to the pillow the night she'd left had said only that she'd been planning to go for a while. The humiliation of that, the fact that he had laughed with and made love to a woman who hadn't really cared, scalded. He'd been a fool, but even worse, he hadn't seen the hurt that had lain in store for his kids.

Rocking his daughter, Sam whispered to her softly. He loved her, she was the most special girl in the whole wide world. He even told her that Donna loved her and just couldn't be here with her, and he forgave himself for the lie. Annie needed that solace, and the truth be damned.

Brushing back the damp curls that had gotten caught in her tears, he waited until her sobs subsided into snuffles and then into the long, even breathing of sleep. Then Sam carried Annie upstairs and tucked her into bed. He followed the sound of giggles, looking for his babies.

Right now, the twins needed him. But come nightfall when the kids were asleep, he was going to have to rethink his family's situation. It had been a year since Donna had gone, granting him sole custody. Time had passed. Still, it was clear now that time alone wasn't helping Annie get past the loss of her mother. He needed to figure out what *would* help.

But for now... Sam walked into the cavernous white kitchen.

"Dee!" Zach called, stumbling away from Mrs. Nelson and toward his father just as fast as his chubby legs could carry him.

Scooping up a twin in each arm, Sam hugged Zach and Janey to him. His quiet little daughter formed her lips into an O and aimed a wet kiss at Sam's cheek.

"Did you two little imps have a good day?" he asked.

"Goo," Janey agreed, smiling up at him as he snuggled her and Zach close, then let them go back to their game.

Okay, the twins *were* doing all right. But then, they'd hardly known Donna. They hadn't reached the age of wondering about their mother's absence. But someday... hell, someday it would happen. When it did, he wanted their world to be so secure that their lives would still be filled with rainbows.

Up until now he hadn't made any major changes in his kids' lives because, well—dammit, losing a mother *was* a major change. Uprooting them would have been wrong. But now, maybe—maybe it was finally time to go home. The thought swirled into Sam's mind and caught there, refusing to budge. It had been years since he'd lived in Tucker, but he'd always loved the town even if it was where he'd met and married Donna. It had become his home from the minute he'd walked into town and—

Sam's attention was diverted by Zach sliding his diapered bottom under the kitchen table as he peeped out from beneath the maze of chairs. "Wuv, Dee," he said, smacking his rosebud lips and throwing kisses.

Chuckling at his son's antics, Sam hunkered down beside him. "I love you too, tiger," he agreed. "Absolutely."

And that was exactly what he was thinking two weeks later as he prepared to climb into his truck. God, he loved his kids. How could he be thinking of leaving them even for a few days?

"I'll be back soon," he told the twins. He hugged them hard, not wanting to let go.

"Soon, pumpkin," he repeated to a wide-eyed, worried Annie, as he gathered her little twig of a body close. "I promise I'll send for you as soon as I find us a new home."

Sam hoped his smile hid the lump the size of Rhode Island located in his throat. He'd never been apart from his kids. If Annie started to cry, he wasn't sure he could leave her.

"Is Tucker far, Daddy?" she asked with a quavering voice.

"Not far, sweetheart. It's still in Illinois. But smaller—and greener. Your uncle Hal lives there—just like I did when I was a teenager. It's a very nice place. Special."

It was. That was why he was going—to find a house that was a home, not just a decorator's dream like this one. And a town where people stayed for lifetimes, not just years.

He was finally going back to help his uncle run the family lumberyard. And there was a strong sense of right about what he was doing, Sam thought, driving away with one last long look in the rearview mirror. But a town, a home and a job weren't enough. His kids also needed someone who could fill the empty holes their mother had left. Someone special had to care for them when he was working—not just a housekeeper. Annie needed a role model, a cheerleader, someone who knew how to turn tears into giggles.

"Rachel Allyn." Sam muttered the name of the woman he'd decided upon, as he passed another mileage marker. His sister, Kate, who maintained her friendship with Rachel, his contacts in town and his memories, assured him that she was the right woman for the job. But there was still one thing Sam wasn't sure of. Would she be willing to help him?

"Dammit." He blew out a long breath, remembering Rachel. Tall, with dark hair and huge gray eyes, she'd been his sister's friend, warm and welcoming to the world...and chilly as November to him. When he'd tried to be nice, she'd slipped away, and when she couldn't do that, she had a cache of comments that went straight for the jugular, but... she'd truly been a wonder with kids. Whether it was her own brothers and sisters or the sticky-faced children she baby-sat for, she'd loved every one of them, flaws and all. She'd bandaged their scraped knees and swung them in great, looping circles. More important, she'd made them laugh. Always.

He knew she was still there, in Tucker. In fact, he knew exactly where to find her.

Still, Sam couldn't ignore the fact that Rachel had always looked at him as though he spent his spare time kicking defenseless animals. And the last time he'd seen her, at his wedding, when everyone had danced with the bride and groom, Rachel had settled into the circle of his arms, then pulled back and walked away, leaving him confused... and mad as hell.

Thinking back, Sam couldn't help smiling at what he must have looked like with his arms looped around a mass of air. It had been a sobering moment for a man who wasn't used to having a woman say no.

But as he drove closer to Tucker, his amusement didn't last long. The fact was that Rachel hadn't even wanted to dance with him back then. Was she going to be willing to care for his children now?

Sam didn't know, but heck, he knew one thing. In just a short time he was going to come face-to-face with Rachel

Allyn for the first time in ten years. This time he didn't intend to be left holding air.

"Hal, good news," Rachel declared as her boss walked into the office of Grayson Lumber. "Lots of good news. My roses are blooming, it's warm, it's sunny, the sky's a perfect blue, and... I just this minute finally found that lousy two thousand dollars we lost on the Jensen account. *Someone* keyed it into the wrong file." She smiled, shaking her head at Hal. He was notorious for messing with her files when she was out of the office.

Rachel waited for Hal's answer, but he just stood there grinning at her. The few strands of gray hair he still had were standing up where he had pushed a hand across his scalp.

"Aw, forget that account," he finally said. "And everything else. I just got a call—from Sam. He's coming home. Right now!"

The stack of papers beneath Rachel's fingers shifted violently as she jerked back at Hal's words.

"Sam?" she asked, sucking in air.

Hal waved one hand impatiently. "My nephew, Rachel. Sam Grayson. Don't you remember him?"

Oh, yes, she remembered. That wasn't the problem. The problem was that she'd thought he was gone forever, and now...

Now, nothing, she thought. Nothing had changed. She still had her flowers, her friends and the same dazzling sky as this morning. So what if Sam Grayson was coming back to town? It was nothing to her.

"I'm happy for you, Hal," Rachel said quietly, and she was. Hal had been all alone since his wife died. Sam and his sister Kate were all the family he had. As part owner of Grayson Lumber, there was no reason in the world Sam shouldn't be coming back to Tucker—and no reason she should be unsettled by the news.

But then Sam had always managed to unsettle her. Even the first time she'd met him and Kate when he'd moved to Tucker from Texas and her mother had gone to clean house for the Graysons.

She had tried to ignore the attraction. At eighteen, Sam was out of reach. His family owned the lumberyard while hers barely owned shoes and socks. Besides, Sam was dating beautiful Donna, and fifteen-year-old Rachel already knew about impossible dreams. Neither her father nor her stepfather had ever seemed to realize that wives and children needed love.

So Rachel had known not to dream about Sam. No way would she repeat her mother's mistakes. Her life had not been pretty back then, but her thoughts had always been lovely. There was a shining world out there and plenty of happiness to be had—as long as she didn't set her sights on the wrong dreams.

"You still with me, Rachel?" Hal asked, and she looked up, embarrassed to be caught remembering. "That Engalls boy didn't upset you, did he? I heard you had a date last night."

Rachel smiled at Hal's choice of words. She shook her head disbelievingly, sending her long, dark hair tumbling over one shoulder. Bob Engalls was thirty years old, not a boy, even if he was sweet and shy.

"Bob's a very nice *man,* Hal," she said, grinning openly.

Hal's brows beetled suddenly. "Darn it, Rachel, you say that about everybody. Hell, *I'm* nice and I'm sixty-eight. Eighty-year-old Jim Hanks is nice, too, but you darn well wouldn't be marrying either of us. 'Very nice' is what you said about that Don Bowers, the one who told everyone he'd be back to ask you to marry him again *this* year. Come on,

Rachel. I want to hear some wedding bells before I'm too old to dance."

Rachel couldn't hold back her laughter. She shook her head at Hal as she leaned forward on her desk. "Don't worry, Hal. I promise you that I'll provide you with a whole day of dancing—someday. But give me some time to find the real thing. I'm not going to marry someone just so you can twirl Lily Dawson around the dance floor."

Hal's face turned pink at Rachel's reference to the lady in question. She really shouldn't tease him. He was such an old sweetheart, a kind boss who'd given her plenty of time off when she'd needed to care for her terminally ill mother two years ago. Now, when he was so excited over Sam's return, it was her turn to be understanding.

"Come on, Hal, we better clean up some of this sawdust before your Sam gets here," she said gently, rising to her feet. "And don't worry about me. I'll fall in love when the right man comes along. I'm sure of it."

And she was. The man who could make her heart do a tango was waiting out there. Somewhere. She'd wanted it to be Don. He'd been warm and funny and patient when he'd passed through town last year, hopeful that she'd learn to love him in time. Maybe she would. When he returned, maybe she'd look at him and feel stars shining inside herself. It could happen, it had *already* happened once—but, of course, that had been the wrong man.

Sam. The name racketed through her brain as she moved around the room with Hal, straightening things that didn't really need straightening.

Sam had been a mistake. She'd known better, but his smile, his displaced Texas drawl, had done terrible, wonderful things to her heart. He'd been kind; she'd almost thought he cared... until she'd overheard a conversation between Sam and Donna. That was when she'd realized Sam thought of her as a needy kid. He felt sorry for her. It was the day Rachel started avoiding Sam—and courting his anger to avoid his pity.

His wedding day had been the worst. By then she'd reached her seventeenth birthday. Not wanting to look conspicuous by being different, she'd agreed to dance with him. She'd started unwillingly into his arms—until she'd felt the brief touch of his hand at her waist. The rush of longing had threatened to betray her. She'd barely been able to walk away.

Rachel touched a petal of one of the carnations on her desk. Sam probably didn't even remember. That was a long time ago. Past history—as was Sam.

"When's he coming, Hal? Will he—bring his children?" The words slipped out even though she didn't want to think about babies with Sam's blue eyes. Children were and always had been her weakness. Their honesty, their innocence, their dirty little faces and sweet smiles always did her in. The combination of Sam and kids—Rachel forced that thought away.

Hal looked up and smiled. "When? Oh, he'll be here pretty soon. Today. The kids will come later, but *Sam* will be here sooner than you think."

Sooner than I want, Rachel thought. But she couldn't say that and didn't want to pursue that line of thought, anyway. It was too fine a day to waste her thoughts on a man who no longer mattered.

Rachel sat down at her desk and turned back to her computer. She breathed in the soothing scent of wood shavings, determined to restore her former good mood.

Hey, yesterday was gone, just like her adolescent crush on Sam. Her life was rich with friends and family. Her days were fun. . . satisfying. She was a woman who'd always known her future was filled with intriguing possibilities.

And Sam was—just an embarrassing glitch in her past. No way was she going to give the man another thought.

Shaking her head at her ridiculous skittishness, Rachel went back to work with a smile. She looked out the window and saw that the day was still blue and perfect. The arrival of a single long-lost man wasn't even going to make a dent in her good mood.

Rachel was bent over a cabinet, filing invoices, when she heard footsteps behind her. Turning slowly, she looked up...and found herself staring right into Sam Grayson's intensely blue eyes.

"Sam..." Her voice faltered. How had the man gotten in here without Hal giving her any warning? And where *was* Hal, anyway?

Stepping back, she took a long, deep breath, studying him even as he stared at her. The years had changed him. The muscles beneath his blue shirt were clearly defined, his thighs were more powerful. He wore blue jeans that had faded nearly to white around the zipper, emphasizing his masculinity. Sam had clearly left his teens behind.

Swallowing, Rachel slid her gaze from his zipper, seeking the safer territory north of Sam's crotch. She noticed that his black hair had early traces of silver at the temples now, but it looked good on him. *He looked good.* Too bad. She had thought that time might have turned him fat and dumpy.

"Hello, Rachel. It's been a long time," he finally said, and his voice reminded her of...yesterday. Deep and husky, it had always felt like a stroke against her feverish skin. She bit back a curse, focusing on the Stetson hat he was dangling from one finger.

"Hi, Sam. Nice hat. Maybe you're passing through on your way home to Texas?" she asked hopefully.

Sam leaned against her desk, his long legs stretched out before him. He plunked his hat down dead center in the middle of her paperwork, then locked his gaze with hers.

"I see time hasn't changed you, Rachel. You're still just as sweet as ever. But don't get your hopes up about Texas. Haven't you heard? I'm coming back to haunt you."

Unable to look away, Rachel took a deep, shuddering breath. How absolutely aggravating that Sam still had the ability to affect her respiration. And it sounded like he really *was* here to stay. This wasn't just a brief family reunion.

"So you're really moving home," she said, hoping she sounded flippant enough. "I'm surprised I hadn't heard anything until today..." She kept her gaze dead-on his, trying to hide her uncertainty about what was going on. Why was Sam coming home after all these years, and why was he in here talking to her of all people when Hal was—where in the world *was* Hal? She craned her neck, trying to see out the window.

A slow smile lifted one corner of Sam's lips. "Don't worry, he's still there, Rachel. We've been outside talking, and we'll talk again in a little while. I'm having dinner with him tonight to discuss how I can help him in the operations of Grayson Lumber. As for not hearing sooner, well, I just didn't want any fanfare. I asked Uncle Hal not to say anything. He wasn't even sure when I was coming until this morning."

Rachel wished he was talking to Hal and not her at this very minute. She braced her palms on the legs of her jeans in an effort to keep her hands still. She didn't want to make polite conversation with Sam Grayson. She especially didn't like the nervous, trembly sensations that were coursing through her body, making her feel like she needed to lean against something—or someone.

Clearing her throat, she plucked a pen from her desk. She twisted the cap off, then snapped it back on again. "Why, Sam? You've been gone a long time. Why bother to come back now?" she asked, trying to sound as casual as possible.

Sam raised one eyebrow, and Rachel wondered if she was being too personal. Did she have a right to ask those kinds of questions? Wouldn't anyone want to know?

Shrugging, Sam watched her restless movements as she capped and uncapped the pen. She froze, realizing that she was fidgeting.

"Times have changed. I'm not a wild teenager anymore, Rachel. I have children," he said, pulling a picture from his wallet and handing it to her. "Right now they need stability. Janey and Zach, the twins, need room to run, and Annie—" Sam cleared his throat and slid one hand across his jaw. "Annie needs much more than she has right now."

Rachel tried not to notice the look of concern that crossed Sam's face. It reminded her too much of how good he had been to *her* when she'd first met him. She had thought it was because there was something special between them, until—she wasn't going to think about that now.

Staring at the snapshot, Rachel saw three little darlings smiling back at her. The twins, with bright, liquid brown eyes, and dimples that dented their chubby cheeks. And the child with big blue eyes and a sober little heart-shaped face had to be the one he'd called Annie. Blue glasses sat crookedly on her nose, and Rachel had an irresistible urge to gently place them back where they belonged. Her heart dropped into a free-fall as she looked at those babies. These were Sam's children, his own flesh. He loved them, it was clear, and he was bringing them back to Tucker, where she would see them all the time. She would see *Sam* all the time...every day, and that was the last thing she wanted.

She'd spent years pushing the man to the back of her mind, and that was where she intended for him to stay.

Stealing one last look at Sam's children, Rachel returned the picture to him. Long seconds of silence stretched out.

"They're beautiful, Sam, and I can understand why you'd want them to grow up in a place like Tucker. Still, that doesn't explain one thing," she finally said, scratching one unpolished nail carefully along the rimmed edge of the desk. "You're here in town, but...why are you *here?*" She looked around the cramped and cluttered office.

He tilted his head to one side. His blue eyes narrowed as if he didn't really like that question. "I'm part owner of this place, remember? With all the expansion Uncle Hal's been planning, he could use another set of hands to help him run the yard."

"Yes, but your uncle is outside. I'm the only one in the office, and you and I both know that we—well, you can't blame me for wondering why you'd want to talk to *me.*"

A sudden image of the way Sam had looked as she'd left him standing empty-armed on a crowded dance floor pushed into Rachel's thoughts. She would have sworn Sam was not the type to hold a grudge, but as he'd said, times had changed.

"Maybe you wanted something from the files?" she asked hopefully, when he didn't answer right away.

Sam straightened up slowly. He raised one eyebrow and held out his hands, like a man asking a woman for a dance.

Rachel felt her face growing warm.

He lowered his hands and smiled slightly. "No, Rachel. I don't need any files, but it looks to me like you need a break," Sam said. "Let me take you out for a soda. For old times' sake."

For old times' sake. But there were no "old times." Not between her and Sam, anyway. Rachel started to shake her head, but she realized that several contractors had walked in the door. She also remembered that Sam was her employer.

"I don't think that's a good idea," she still managed to say, standing her ground. Several more men had come in, curious about the man who would also be giving the orders from now on, she imagined. They were milling around and pretending to be reading the signs on the wall, the same signs that had been hanging there for at least five years.

Sam looked at them, then targeted her with his bright blue gaze.

"We've got business that has nothing to do with Grayson Lumber, Rachel. I've got a good reason for darkening your door, but I'd rather not take it up here. How about you?"

Sam had moved closer, so that he couldn't be heard. He was still a good six inches behind her, but close enough that Rachel could feel him there. A shiver ran through her. "It's not my lunch hour yet," she said quietly.

"It is now," he insisted, taking her arm. She felt the warmth of his fingers as he touched her skin. Shock waves ran through her as she registered the first and only physical contact she'd had with Sam since that dance years ago. She realized just as quickly that he had pulled his hand away. Looking up at him, she saw that he was frowning. He'd shoved his hand deep into his pocket.

"You can always change your mind, Sam. I won't tell," she whispered back, grasping for false courage and raising one brow as he motioned her toward the door.

"Lady, when I start something I finish it, whether it's a job, a conversation or a dance."

His last words were low and husky, a whisper meant for Rachel's ears only. Her breath caught in her throat, but before she knew it, she had been whisked past the men standing closest to the door. She found herself alone in a pickup truck with Sam Grayson, and she realized she'd never really been alone with him in her life. There were no barriers to latch on to this time.

Chapter Two

Sam studied Rachel from the corner of his eye as they rode in silence toward the park two miles outside of town. No one would be there in this afternoon heat. They could talk in private; he could be as frank as he needed to be.

That was good, that privacy, because Rachel was just as bold, just as sassy as she'd always been. She was also just as lovely as ever. More so. As a teenager she'd been thin, almost too thin. Now she was all soft curves, all rose-kissed satin skin. Her dark, shining hair fell over her shoulders and rested on the slopes of her breasts. Those long legs of hers would make most men slide off the road if they stared at them the way he was staring right now. But, of course, he wasn't affected, Sam knew, giving the wheel a sharp jerk—because this was Rachel Allyn, and his friendship with her had died on the vine years ago.

That didn't matter. He and Rachel didn't have to be tight for what he had in mind. She just had to care for his kids. That was the only important issue here, and he knew that he wouldn't have a problem with that. Rachel was the original earth mother where children were concerned. It was a fact that he'd fought to deny endless times in the past week...but one that kept sliding into his thoughts each time he'd hugged Annie and felt the desperation in her thin little arms. She needed someone who understood little girls—someone who loved kids and accepted them for what they were.

And much as he hated to admit it, Sam couldn't deny the genuine longing in Rachel's eyes when she'd looked at his children's picture. He remembered years ago, watching her running with her little sisters and brothers, hugging them up and swinging them around till they all lay down on the ground, dizzy and exhausted and giggling. She'd kissed away their tears, held them close and tight when they'd needed it. She'd helped them with their homework, sang them songs, she'd shared her smiles with them. It was only he who had always invited her cynicism and displeasure. She had usually made an excuse to leave whenever he'd been around, and he could only imagine what she must be feeling now that he'd forced her hand.

Glancing to the side again, he saw that Rachel had pressed herself up against the door. Sam didn't know what it was about himself that had always made Rachel skittish, but he was sorry that he had made that crack about dancing now.

"If you're worried that I'm going to throw you out of a moving truck, you can calm down right now, Rachel. It's taking all my concentration just to navigate this bumpy road. Besides, I never had much use for men who manhandled women."

Rachel had the grace to look embarrassed. "I wasn't worried that you were going to kill me by shoving me out the door, Sam. Although if you wanted to *dance* me over a cliff, I might understand. I—I'm sorry about your wedding. I didn't mean to embarrass you and—well, it was a long time ago. But I *am* sorry."

Sam pulled up at the park entrance and stopped the truck. He eased his long legs out, then came around to help Rachel down. She was already closing the door. He shrugged. "You're right. It *was* a long time ago, Rachel. And right now I'm just hoping we can put the past in the past and concentrate on something else. Something more important."

Rachel hugged her elbows close. "Like what, Sam? What is it that's so important you couldn't ask me back at the yard?"

Stepping closer, Sam locked his gaze onto hers. Her eyes were gray and waif big, nervous, but he wouldn't let her look away. "My kids are what's important. At least to me, Rachel. Only them. They're all that matters to me, and they're lost and unsure since their mother left. I'm willing to do anything I can, whatever is necessary to see that they're happy. That's what this is about, Rachel."

Rachel frowned. "I understand your concern for your children, but—" She held out her hands, clearly confused.

Sam tucked his thumbs in the back of his belt, he spread his feet wide, prepared for battle. "I believe that you're a person who might be able to help me. That is, if you're willing."

When Rachel opened her mouth, Sam held up one hand to stop whatever objection she might make. "Hear me out, Rachel. My children—the twins are too young to remember their mother, but Annie... one minute she was a happy little girl, the next minute her mother had vanished into thin air. Donna left a note, but it wasn't the kind of thing that would help a little girl understand how her mother could leave her. What *could* help? She's scared and way too sad now and getting worse. She's finally realized that her mother isn't coming back, and she watches me, petrified, as if she's afraid that I'll disappear, too. No matter how much I assure her that I'll never leave her, I know it's not enough. She needs more—a real home, good friends, a father *and* a woman who can reassure her and be a role model."

Rachel looked up at Sam. His eyes were like blue fire, gazing into her soul, and she was suddenly afraid of what was coming. It wouldn't be something she would like, she was sure of that.

She wanted to leave and actually did take a step back, but then Sam reached out. He touched her hand with his own, and the unexpected contact stopped her retreat completely.

"I realize it's asking a lot, Rachel, knowing how you feel about me, but I want you to think about something. I'd like you to consider coming to work for me. Come take care of my children. They need someone like you. Desperately. You're a natural with kids. You would be good for them. So, I'm humbling myself, Rachel. I'm asking you now to put away the past and consider helping me raise my children. I'm asking if you would think about it."

Rachel couldn't break away from Sam's blue gaze. He had loved a woman who'd left him, and all he had left in life now were his children. He would do anything for them. He would obviously even apply to a woman he didn't really care for.

"I already have a job, Sam."

"Not like this one."

She breathed in deeply, filling her lungs. Oh, he was right. So very right. This job would mean being around Sam all the time, living in his shadow much more than working at the lumberyard would. There was no way she could even consider it, not when just looking at the man made her dizzy.

"This job you're talking about—" she began.

"Would mean commitment, a great deal of commitment, Rachel. I'd want them to be able to think of you as someone they could count on. But I'd also offer what I could. Absolute financial security, I'd even help out with your own brothers and sisters if they ever needed it. That's a lot more than the job at the lumberyard offers."

He was right. It was. It was also a hell of a lot more dangerous than the job at the lumberyard.

"You've come all this way to ask for my help?" Rachel took a deep breath and blew it out. "I think—this is crazy, Sam."

There was only a slight hesitation. "That's right. It's crazy, but I'm still making the offer."

She looked up at him then—dared to stare straight into those fearsome blue eyes of his. "Forgive me for thinking that this seems a little irresponsible of you, Sam, but you're basing your assumptions on a girl you knew ten years ago. How do you know I'd be good for your children? How do you know I haven't changed?"

There, she had him. This would make him think, make him back down so that she had room to think herself. With a little time and courage, she could catch her breath and tell him what she should already have said: she couldn't possibly even consider his offer. She could forget that little angel with the blue glasses, and the break in Sam's voice when he'd told about Annie waiting for him to vanish in the night. She could forget that her own childhood had been scary at times.

But Sam wasn't speaking. Instead he was pulling a slip of paper from his pocket. A well-worn paper filled with scribbles.

"I'll confess that I fought against turning to you, Rachel. You and I don't exactly have a shining history. So I made some calls, half hoping I'd find someone else. I told people I was a businessman passing through town and that I needed the best child care available for my children. Not a single person hesitated to give me your name. You topped the list every time. No one else even came close. So, are you going to tell me you've developed a sudden aversion to children, Rachel?"

"I'm telling you that I have a life of my own, Sam. A job of my own."

"I've talked to Hal. He thinks this might be good for you."

Rachel crossed her arms, took a deep breath. "The man thinks you're only a hair away from sprouting wings, Sam. You're his only living relative other than Kate. If you said it was a good idea to torch Grayson Lumber, Hal would be lighting the match right now. What did you expect him to say?"

Sam smiled, the corners of his mouth drifting up, and Rachel cursed her heart that started tripping away at double time.

"I expected him to tell me that I was springing this on you too suddenly."

Rachel nodded her head. Her mind was still spinning from Sam's unexpected proposition.

"And I expected him to suggest that I was being presumptuous."

Rachel opened her eyes wide. Sam didn't sound especially repentant.

"And I expected him to tell me that I'd be incredibly lucky if you didn't kick me in the shins."

"The day isn't over yet," she said, trying not to smile at the man's utter audacity. "But as we said, a lot of years have passed, Sam. I'm an adult and I don't kick, hit or throw things. Still, I wasn't lying, Sam. I do have a life of my own, one I'm already committed to."

"Those guys Uncle Hal tells me you've been dating. Are you considering marriage anytime soon? Maybe moving away?"

Rachel nearly gasped and jumped back when Sam took a step forward, breath close. "That's none of your business, Sam, but even if I was contemplating marriage tomorrow, it's not the problem here." It *wasn't* the problem, but at the moment Rachel wished it was. If she was waltzing down the aisle tomorrow, she wouldn't be standing here with Sam today.

"So explain the situation to me, Rachel." Sam's voice was a whisper, his lips were way too close.

The trouble was that if she committed herself to Sam, she would have to put off one of her dreams, her plans of buying and running her own flower shop, a goal she was close to achieving. But more than that, much more than that, was the thought of what working with Sam in his home would be like. They'd have to talk, consult on the kids, see each other in a more personal way than they would at the lumberyard and...Rachel wasn't foolish enough to test her emotions that way. She'd given up on her dreams of Sam long ago. No way would she do anything that might call them forth again. Not in this lifetime. She believed heart and soul that she'd find the man who was meant to be her life's companion. But it would never be Sam. Someone with Sam's qualities, maybe, but—not Sam. She shook her head. "No, I can't do this, Sam."

"My children need you," Sam coaxed, his voice low and husky and urgent.

"Give yourself time. You'll find a woman, one you'll love and maybe even want to marry, someone who would be a wife to you and an actual mother to your children."

Sam shook his head angrily. "I'm not going down that road again, Rachel. Love, a wife and marriage, that's out of the question as far as I'm concerned. But my children do need someone to care for and help them, and I don't have the luxury of time. Annie's heart is breaking now. What I need is not a woman for myself, but a woman who'll help me mend Annie's world."

Rachel bit her lip. She thought of that picture of those babies. She thought of Sam trying to raise his kids alone all his life because of one woman's betrayal. And those children with no mother. She'd feel for them; she knew that she would. A long time ago she'd learned that telling herself not to feel just wasn't enough, and she didn't want to go down that path again. She didn't really even want to risk meeting Sam's kids. She certainly didn't want to risk being around *him*. Sam had dazzled and blinded her before, and when the man that was really right for her came along, she didn't want to miss him because her eyes were turned in Sam's direction. It was too much to ask of herself.

Turning around, Rachel retraced her steps as she walked away from Sam. She swung back the door of the truck. "I promise you, Sam, that I would help you if I could, but—"

Sam uttered a word that Rachel was sure he never used in front of his kids. "I'm sorry, Rachel. Forget that I asked. It was stupid of me to even suggest such a thing. I knew that."

"No, Sam, I—I'd like to see your children happy, but this—it just wouldn't work."

Crawling back into the truck, Rachel took deep breaths and closed her eyes as she listened to the sound of Sam shutting the door and revving up the engine. She counted the minutes till she could be home and able to let her emotions have free rein. At least she had gotten through this. At least Sam had asked, she had answered, and everything was over. She had been given the opportunity to share a tiny corner of

Sam's life and she had passed on it. The danger of giving in to temptation had slipped by. She was safe.

"Damn!"

Sam sat on the lumpy bed in his room at the Tuckered Out Motel, contemplating this afternoon. He'd really made a mess of things this time. But then, what had he expected? Had he really thought that Rachel's eyes would light up when part of the bargain he was offering her included spending a certain amount of time with him?

Just what kind of a bargain *had* he offered her, anyway?

Come take care of my kids, because I need you to, Rachel. Because I want you to, Rachel.

He was sure someone who looked like Rachel Allyn had received a lot more enticing offers than his. Why on earth would she want to take on the care and feeding of a family when she'd been the sole care giver of her ailing mother before Lucy Allyn's death eighteen months ago? After being tied to home during that time, Rachel was probably enjoying the freedom of her life-style these days. He couldn't say that he blamed her much, either.

"Nice going, Grayson," he said with a sneer. "Just be glad the lady didn't laugh in your face."

So, he thought, prying off his boots and stretching out on the sloping length of the bed, he'd struck out. Completely. But then, that came as no surprise. If he had any sense at all, and he liked to think he did, he'd give up this ridiculous quest. He'd find a house, he'd hire someone who knew how to cook, at least better than he did, and he'd try once again, by smothering his children with love, to fill the void Donna's departure had left. Surely this small and safe town, his love and time would do the trick. Annie would surely smile again someday soon. He didn't need Rachel Allyn. More important, he didn't want her. He wasn't even going to think of her anymore.

Sam had repeated those phrases a dozen times and had just about convinced himself that he wasn't really quitting too quickly, when the phone rang.

"Hell," he said, nearly rolling off the sloping bed in his haste to pick up the receiver. "Hello."

"Daddy?" The quavery little voice on the end couldn't have been smaller—or more dear to him.

"Hey, pumpkin? How's my best big girl doing? Are you taking care of yourself and eating everything Mrs. Nelson puts in front of you?"

"Daddy," Annie drawled. "Mrs. Nelson made rutabagas with dinner. I don't even like the *word* rutabaga, but you don't have to worry. I made Janey and Zach eat some, 'cause they are little and they must get all their vitamins."

"Hon-ey, Annie," Sam said. "What did we talk about earlier? Your job is just to take good care of Annie. Mrs. Nelson is there to do the rest."

A long silence met this statement. Sam propped himself up on one elbow. "Annie? You there, hon?"

"But Zach and Janey like only me to put them to bed, Daddy. Mrs. Nelson doesn't sing, not like Mommy always did."

Sam's heart nearly broke at this statement. Annie was singing to her brother and sister, but who was singing for Annie? He'd tried once or twice, but it had only seemed to make her miss her mother more.

"That's good, then, sweetheart," he assured her. "I'm glad you sang for them."

"Daddy?" the little voice cut in, so tiny he could barely hear her.

"What, pumpkin? You just say what you want."

"Will you be coming back for us soon, Daddy? Please."

Sam swallowed back the lump that surged to his throat. He cursed the miles that separated him from his child, but he didn't want his Annie's first glimpse of Tucker to be this run-down motel, the only place he could stay besides the room Hal lived in above the lumberyard office. He had to have the right place, someplace bright and sparkling and warm. A place where Annie would feel safe and welcomed.

"I'll be coming for you just as soon as I can get settled in, Annie. I promise you it won't be long, not long at all. I miss you, pumpkin."

"Me too, Daddy. And don't worry about the babies. I'll let them know that you'll send for us soon, and I'll make sure they eat their vegetables every day."

As he promised to call back later that night and returned the phone to its cradle, Sam closed his eyes. He guessed he was a liar, after all. Because he *did* need Rachel Allyn. He very definitely needed her for Annie, and he'd do whatever was necessary to convince the woman that he and his children were a good bargain—even if he had to crawl on his knees and triple her salary.

Sam got to Grayson Lumber a few minutes later than he'd planned the next day. He'd spent more time fighting the uncooperative mattress and his own thoughts last night than he had sleeping, and when he'd finally succumbed to exhaustion, it had taken some heavy-duty sunlight to awaken him. He'd hoped to catch Rachel before she made it into the office. Instead he could see through the glass of the door that she already had her beautiful face turned toward the computer on her desk. She was smiling. Good. Maybe his timing wasn't so bad after all.

Nodding a greeting to two smiling grandmothers passing by, Sam shoved open the office door. He watched Rachel as he moved closer to her desk. Unconsciously she pushed one slender hand through her hair, letting the dark satiny stuff fall in careless abandon about her face. She scrunched her brow, frowning suddenly, then reached out to fiddle gently with the stems of the flowers on her desk. Bloodred salvia, the flaming color stood out against Rachel's pale skin. She cradled the blossoms against her palm, studying them as if the key to the universe lay in those flowers. Then suddenly she turned back to the computer, striking a few keys.

"Hah, gotcha, you little devil," she said, sitting back in triumph.

"Problems, Rachel?" Sam said quietly.

She jerked her chin up quickly as if a puppet master had yanked an invisible string attached to her head. Her movement emphasized her long, slender neck and the soft shadows revealed by the deep vee of her ivory blouse.

"I—Sam, you startled me. I thought I was alone," she confessed. "And no, not problems, really. Just one of those pesky little accounting figures that had been eluding me all morning. I finally figured out where I'd lost it."

"You get the answers to your accounting questions from flowers?" he asked, nodding toward the plant.

She shrugged self-consciously and ran her hand through her hair again. "I'm a sucker for flowers," she admitted sheepishly. "They're very...soothing."

So stubborn Rachel had a soft spot for flowers. Flowers *and* children, Sam thought. It fit somehow, touched something deep inside him, and he reminded himself again that *he* was the one who had always brought out the fight in Rachel. He'd have to remember that and see what he could do about it.

Rachel bit her lip. She looked up at Sam expectantly. "Are you looking for Hal?" she asked, not bothering to disguise the hope in her voice.

Sam felt a trace of annoyance shoot through him. He forced it back, twisted his lips up in a smile. "Nice try, Rachel, but no, I'm not looking for Hal. I came to apologize to you."

Blinking, Rachel looked away and stared longingly at the vase of flowers. Gently he pushed it toward her.

"Go ahead, touch them if it will make getting through this any easier for you. I know you considered me a closed chapter after yesterday. And I just want you to know that my offer— I never intended to be so blunt or pushy. I didn't mean to use you."

Rachel stopped squeezing the vase she now held between her cupped hands. "That's a lie, Sam."

He considered her words, then nodded. He placed his hands on his hips and let his chin drop toward his chest. "It's a lie," he admitted. "I need you right now. I'm worried about Annie. Hell, I'm scared silly about her, and I guess I'd do about anything—lie, cheat, steal, turn my sister's best friend into a slave—I'd do all that to help my daughter. But heck, Rachel, I didn't intend to insult you by coming on so strong." Sighing, he looked up, ran one hand over his jaw.

To his surprise Rachel rose to her feet and stepped around the desk. She reached out, hesitated, then gently touched his sleeve. It was barely a feather of a touch, yet he felt it dead center in the core of him. It burned him down to his boots.

He looked deep into her wide gray eyes and saw that she was fighting her own nervousness, yet she had still not moved her hand away. "I don't know how to say this, but it wasn't that you were so pushy or that I was insulted by your arrogance, Sam. It's just—you—me?" She held her hands out helplessly. He knew what she was thinking. They'd probably start a cold war within the first week.

Rachel stood there looking at Sam, waiting for him to speak. She shouldn't have touched him, but he had looked so very lost when he'd spoken of his Annie. The woman within her just hadn't been able to turn away. Now, however, with her hand resting on his sleeve, feeling coursed through her, feeling that went well beyond simple friendly concern. Carefully she opened her palm and let go.

"It's not me that I would expect you to relate to, Rachel. Just my children. I'd make it worth your while."

No, oh, no he wouldn't. He'd admitted he wanted her for his children's sake. If she was just as honest, she'd admit that Sam could still make her nerves vibrate just by opening his mouth. That was what it would be like, being around him, and nothing was worth that kind of risk. If she was smart, she'd send him elsewhere—pronto.

Scrambling for the distancing demeanor she'd always used to deal with Sam, Rachel searched for cool and clever words, then looked into the man's eyes. Damn. She couldn't do it this time. She couldn't attack him with words or even make a quick and quiet exit. This was Sam, and he had been through hell in the last year. He had lost the woman he'd loved, was crazy with worry about his kids. No wonder he had turned to her. The man was obviously not thinking clearly. He was hurting. Her own ego, the knowledge that Sam had only sought her out because he was desperate—she had to ignore that now. Retaliating with words was not allowed this time.

"I can't do what you're asking, Sam. It's impossible," she repeated softly, ignoring her thumping heartbeat. "But I will help you at least make sure that the children are settled and welcomed in Tucker. I'll be a friendly face to them. I promise you that."

Sam blew out a puff of air and shook his head. "You're a hell of a stubborn woman, Rachel, but—thank you. I'll take you up on that," he said, sliding his hand past her side and plucking a flower from the vase.

He ran one finger along the length of the stem, brushed the pad of his fingertip against the tiny crimson blossoms. "This doesn't mean I'm giving up on the original plan, a commitment to a more secure arrangement, Rachel. I told you I'd commit crimes for Annie's sake. You can't expect me to be less stubborn than you where my daughter's concerned, but for now I'll give in. And thank you for offering to see my kids settled. I want to bring them here as soon as I can, but—" He flailed his hand out to the side, flower and all, in a frustrated gesture.

"But what, Sam?" Rachel rested her hips against the desk, trying not to show how nervous this whole conversation had made her. "You didn't already tell the kids that I would be there waiting for them, did you?" Her voice sounded too high, too loud to be casual.

Grinning suddenly, Sam raised one brow. "I said I was determined that you would, in time, come over to my side, Rachel. I didn't say I was drop-dead stupid. Don't you think I knew that the first words out of your mouth were not going to be, 'Oh yes, Sam, I'll do anything you say'?"

At Sam's expression and pitiful attempt to mimic her higher pitched voice, Rachel couldn't hold back her own smile. "So if you knew I wasn't going to fall prey to your nefarious schemes, Sam, why didn't you just pack up the kids and come on in?"

Sam suddenly sobered. He pushed one hand back through his dark hair in an impatient gesture.

"It's not that simple, Rachel. I stopped by Ben Miller's Realty yesterday and he showed me the old Brenner place. It's what I want, but it's not ready to be lived in. Not yet, anyway."

Rachel knew that was true. She'd driven by there just yesterday.

"I know, but it *is* a wonderful house, Sam. All those turrets and gables and gingerbread. When I was a little girl, I thought it must be a castle. Your Annie's going to feel just like a princess."

Sam studied Rachel as she spoke. Her eyes were glowing with warmth, she was waving her hands around as she talked. And when she finished on a smile, he stared into her face—and stopped breathing for three whole seconds. Rachel, he realized, had never really smiled at him. Not like that. Not in years, anyway. She was like a young girl herself, soft and breathless—and heartbreakingly lovely. For some reason that knowledge made him exceedingly angry.

He managed to nod his head. "Hell, I've got to go," he said suddenly, his voice rough and hard. Quickly he turned toward the door.

As though startled out of a dream, Rachel looked at him with dazed eyes. "Of course, Sam. I never meant to detain you."

"I'm sorry," he said. "Guess I'm acting like a jerk. Don't pay any attention to me." And he meant it. It wasn't her fault that he'd just noticed that elusive Rachel could stop a man's heart mid-beat. It wasn't her fault that desire had lanced through him like a sword. He'd been a long time without a woman's touch—or a woman's smile. It was only natural that he should feel desire when faced with a beauty like the woman standing next to him. But it wasn't her fault.

"I guess I'm just worried about the kids being without me," he explained as he moved away.

But as he neared the door, Sam couldn't keep from turning around one more time. "Rachel? I could—darn, I'd really like a woman's opinion on what I should do about decorating the place. Someone who knows something about kids' tastes."

It was a question, a polite request, hanging between them.

Rachel blew out a breath. She didn't want to go with Sam, but she was impressed by his dedication to his children. And hadn't she said she'd do what she could to help him?

He looked at her expectantly, one brow raised. "No dice, Rachel?"

It was a dare, a not-very-subtle reminder of her promise, a taunting challenge.

"All right, you certainly know how to make a woman feel guilty, Sam," she said with a sigh. "But I don't get off work until four o'clock, and I'm not leaving early today even if you *are* Grayson Lumber. I work until the day is done."

Sam's wicked smile caused the breath to freeze in her lungs. "Four o'clock," he agreed, his words so low that they felt like a caress. "It's a date, Rachel. I'll pick you up then."

Not a date, Rachel thought, as she watched Sam's broad back move away from her. A date was when a man chose a woman because he wanted her, and it would never be that way between her and Sam. He'd already told her what he was looking for, and it was not the pleasure of her company. Still, she'd be waiting just like she'd said she would.

She hoped to heaven she didn't regret this.

Chapter Three

Rachel was just beginning to finally get a grip on herself and settle back to business when she looked up to see one of the men who worked in the yard standing beside her desk. He was holding a package from the only florist in town. He was also grinning ear to ear.

"Somebody sent you flowers, Rachel," he said smugly. "Wonder who these could be from."

Well, he wasn't the only one wondering, Rachel thought, but she had a sneaky suspicion she knew the answer to his question. It had been a while since she'd gotten flowers—Bob was just way too shy, and no one had ever even commented on the blossoms she trucked to work daily—until Sam had asked about them this morning.

Thanking Tom, she waited until he had reluctantly shuffled out before peeling the paper back. Bright white blossoms with yellow centers revealed themselves to her. Dozens of daisies, crowded in an exquisite crystal vase, pure and white and lovely.

Her hand shook as she reached for the card. She had to force herself to open it.

"Thank you, Rachel, for offering your time and for not spitting in my eye the way I know you wanted to. I hope you'll accept these daisies as a sign of friendship and appreciation. Sam," was written in bold, black letters.

Spit in his eye? Had she really looked like that? Most likely, Rachel thought with a smile as she pushed her face up against the soft, gentle daisies. Sam always did bring out her defenses. Still, he'd sent her daisies, her favorites. She somehow thought that the choice of blossoms hadn't been coincidental. Most men would have sent something more exotic automatically, never suspecting how much the innocent freshness of fragile white daisies appealed to her—but Sam had zeroed in on her favorites.

A niggling suspicion formed in the back of Rachel's mind. Sam had said that he would do anything for his child. Did that include bribing her with flowers? She looked at the blossoms that shivered delicately with each waft of air that passed. Yes, she decided, these flowers were probably a bribe.

But a nice one, she admitted with a shrug. Leave it to Sam to hit her hard right where she was the most vulnerable. She would just have to learn to ignore the man.

And that's what she was still trying to do when he showed up at exactly four. Shoving the last scrap of loose paper inside her drawer, Rachel picked up the daisies and headed for the door before Sam could even open it.

"Thank you for the flowers, Sam," she said, helping herself into his truck before he could move to her side, "but they really weren't necessary. I don't spit in people's eyes. At least not on Fridays."

Sam chuckled and took the flowers from her, placing the heavy, leaded vase carefully on the floor beside her feet.

Looking up from his position near her left knee, he smiled up into her eyes.

"And what do you do with your Fridays, Rachel?"

His lips were dangerously near her skin and she felt a crazy, dizzying urge to push closer. But that was silly, foolish, impossible. She thought of the last few Fridays that she'd spent with Bob Engalls. Pleasant evenings when she hadn't felt dizzy at all. Rachel frowned at the thought.

"I bite people's heads off on Fridays, Sam," she said, quickly sliding her knee away from temptation. "So just don't do anything to get me riled."

"I'll remember that," he said quietly and with a smile, and it was clear he was making every effort to be nice as they moved on, finally arriving at the big two-story house with the wraparound porch.

Getting out of the truck, Rachel could feel Sam's every move as he came up behind her and followed her in the door. She masked her reaction by paying attention to the details of the big house that sat on a full acre of land.

"Sam," she whispered. "I've never been *inside* here before. It's—wonderful, a kid's paradise. Just look at the window seats and all the cubbyholes for little people to hide in. And that staircase. I can just see a little girl playing dress up and walking down these stairs in a dress that's three sizes too big," she said, moving up two steps.

When she turned to look, Sam was closer than she'd thought, nearly on eye level. He was staring at her openly. She felt her breath catch in her throat.

"Lady," he whispered. "Kate was right. You're the one. Come—be with us. You—I could help you get that flower shop you want to open."

Rachel let her mouth fall open. An indignant little gasp slipped from her throat. "How did you know about that?"

Sam shrugged, a slight trace of red creeping up from his white shirt collar. "I was grilling Cynthia over at the flower shop about your tastes when I was there earlier. I'm sure she didn't mean to drop your secrets."

"I'm sure that *you* didn't have anything to do with her spilling the beans," Rachel admonished, not sure whether to tell the man off or to laugh at him. He looked so absolutely guilty.

"I might have," he conceded, tucking his thumbs in his jeans. "But now that I know, I could help you. I'd pay you well for your time, Rachel, better than I'm paying you now, and well enough that you could open up your own shop in a nearby town in a few years."

"You think I'd sell myself for a flower shop, Sam?"

Sam frowned, raking one hand through his hair till it stood up in places, making him look frustrated—but still sexy as hell. "Dammit, Rachel, I'm not talking about selling yourself. I'm talking about working for me, staying with my children while they need you, then retiring to the kind of life you truly want. I could make that happen for you. I'd be willing to negotiate the terms."

Rachel closed her eyes. "Sam," she said. "I don't think—"

But Sam reached out and placed two fingers over her lips. "Don't—don't decide right now, Rachel. Wait. Please."

Waiting would be a mistake. Rachel knew that. The thing to do right now was say no, firmly and clearly, and then move far away from Sam so that she couldn't take back her answer. Because she knew the dangers of waiting and spending more time with this man. He always affected her so. She should say no. Immediately.

But when she opened her eyes, she found herself much too close to Sam. And when she opened her mouth, she felt the sensitive flesh of her lips dragging against the pads of

Sam's fingertips—and she found she couldn't breathe. There was no way she could talk.

Still, she managed to shake her head. She read the disappointment in Sam's eyes, and she knew what he was thinking. He didn't want to fail his children again. He was so worried for his kids.

Sam and babies—she turned away from that thought once again. She needed to say something, something that would end all this once and forever.

Stepping away from his touch, Rachel opened her mouth. She looked up into the bluest eyes she'd ever known. Sexy eyes. Worried eyes.

"You'll need help if you're going to whip this house into shape," she whispered, "but we could probably get it livable in two or three days."

Sam's smile was like a touch. Rachel dragged in a deep breath as he moved closer.

"You're an angel," he said in that soft, husky voice of his.

No, she was an idiot. An absolute idiot. But at least if she did this much for Sam, it would be enough. She could walk away from him and get on with her own life without a backward glance.

Sam hammered the last nail into the loose piece of molding around the living room door, then glanced through the doorway into the kitchen. Rachel had finished scrubbing the chrome trim on the stove and was arranging a long drift of philodendron, lifting the heavy rope of leaves and trailing it up and over the front of the plate rack. She'd washed down every visible space, polished every surface, until the place nearly sparkled. She'd also silently slipped out of the room every time he'd entered it.

He watched Rachel as she raised her arms over her head. She fussed with the uncooperative strand of green, hummed a perky little tune. Her hair had been pulled back into a loose ponytail earlier, but the long, dark strands had almost all worked free by now. She had a smudge of dirt the shape of a fuzzy handprint right across her blue denim bottom that was swaying to the music. Grinning, Sam wondered what she'd do if he went over and dusted off her perfect little backside, then mentally swatted himself for the thought.

He was still trying to win Rachel's cooperation for his children's sake. He'd sent her flowers again today. Violets. But that didn't mean he wanted to get close and personal with the lady. Besides, she'd probably just walk away, ignoring his existence the way she had when she was a kid. But, of course, she wasn't a kid anymore. Not even remotely close, Sam thought, studying the curve of her hips as she moved. No, she was clearly an achingly lush and lovely woman now.

Sam shoved his errant and unwelcome thoughts aside. "Let me give you a hand with that," he said, watching as she tried to loop one part of the plant around the edge of the shelf and still keep the rest from falling. "It looks like a two-person job to me."

Rachel stopped moving. She stood frozen for two whole seconds, then turned her head and looked back at him, her gray eyes large and wary. Slowly she raised one shoulder in a shrug. "I'm fine, Sam. Really."

But as she went back to her work, Sam could see her suck in a long breath of air. That confirmed what he had already suspected. Rachel hadn't known that he'd been watching her—and she didn't feel good about it, either.

This was the way it had always been with her. Always had been...and still was. Everyone in town had been glad to see him come home and had told him so—all except for Rachel. She was still ducking around corners where he was concerned, still trying to pretend he didn't exist—and he was damn sick and tired of being the invisible man.

Strolling into the kitchen, Sam came up behind her. Easily he framed her body and reached up to take the plant from her slender grasp.

She stiffened in front of him, becoming ramrod straight, like an icicle in his arms, but he could feel her heart pounding like a sledgehammer. It echoed through her body and resonated into his chest.

"Sam, I told you—"

"Shh, Rachel," he whispered, stilling her attempts to slip away by placing his hand on top of hers. Instantly she froze. "I know what you told me, but I can't stand by and watch you struggle when I can help. You're one hell of a stubborn woman, Rachel Allyn," he declared. "Do you know that?"

She let out a long puff of air. "Well, I guess I do now, Sam." Rachel took another deep breath, still locked in the bracket of Sam's arms. "So," she finally said, turning her head slightly so that the silk of her hair brushed against his lips. "Are we going to just stand here or are we going to get this plant in place?"

It would have been a tough choice if Sam hadn't heard the panic in her voice. Left to his own devices, he might have stood there a few moments longer. The slide of Rachel's hair across his skin, the feel of her slender curves pressed to him—well, it had been a long time since he'd felt raw desire. It didn't make sense to feel this way, since it was Rachel he held in his arms, but it was good to know he could still feel something, even if it was the wrong woman and the wrong time.

"Sam?" Rachel wiggled, trying to get free, and pressed her tight little bottom right up against him. Only a stone man could have controlled himself—or been able to mask the results.

Sam sucked in air, dragging it into his suddenly depleted lungs. Quickly he stepped back and away. "Let's get this done," he said, clearing his voice.

As he held the plant in place and Rachel made sure that it was secured, Sam watched the way she touched the plant, careful not to tear any of the leaves.

Suddenly she stopped what she was doing and stared him straight in the eye. "You've got to stop sending me flowers, Sam."

She had propped one hand on her hip, thinking no doubt that it made her look stern and no-nonsense. In truth, Sam admitted, it only made him think that she had a deliciously curved hip, one made for the fit of a man's hands. He could see, though, how telling her that would be a major big-time mistake. She'd never say yes to his plans if he chased her away by giving in to this damn itch she was calling forth in him. Instead he simply raised one brow and grinned.

"You don't like violets, Rachel?"

Rachel lowered her other hand to her hip. She tried to frown, but he could see the smile trying to peep out from underneath. "You know darn well that I love violets, Sam Grayson," she said, staring him down. "Cynthia admitted that you specifically asked what my favorites are, but that's not the point. The point is that you are clearly trying to bribe me when I've already told you several times that I can't do what you're asking."

"So my attempt at bribery—it's not working?"

Lowering her hands from her hips to run them down the legs of her jeans, Rachel shook her head slowly. "Sam, you know that it's just not possible. It would never work. So you can stop now. You don't need to send me any more flowers."

"You like them though, don't you? Even if they come from me?"

Rachel reached out and touched the tail end of the philodendron. "I like them," she whispered, turning her head away.

She did. Sam knew that much even if he didn't know anything else about Rachel. He didn't know how to convince her to care for his children. He'd never had to work much to win a woman, not even Donna. His wife had sought *him* out, not the other way around. The flowers had been the only way he could think of to coax Rachel. They were the only power he could wield in any form. Any fool could see that she loved green things. A man who wanted to win her to his side would naturally woo her with blossoms. But she'd already said that it would be impossible for him to win this battle, so...he should stop trying. He really should, but he knew he wouldn't. Not yet, anyway.

"When will you be back with the kids?" Rachel asked, stepping back a space.

"Tomorrow. I'm leaving just as soon as I finish up here. I've called Annie ten times in the last two days, but if I don't get there soon...well, I think Mrs. Nelson's ready to walk out the door. Annie decided yesterday that she wanted to learn how to cook. I don't think the first lesson went all that well."

Rachel raised her brows. "Well, she's only six, Sam."

Sam twisted up one side of his mouth and shook his head. "Oh, the problem wasn't with Annie. Not at all. I guess she did just fine for a six-year-old intent on learning it all in one day. But while Mrs. Nelson was explaining the fine points of making a blueberry pie to my six-year-old, the twins got into the containers of blueberries. Major food fight," he concluded.

"Major mess?" Rachel guessed.

Sam nodded. "Annie told me that we now have pretty purple-polka-dotted curtains instead of white ones. Mrs. Nelson's in a bit of a snit. Besides, I miss them. It's time to bring them home."

Realizing he was in danger of opening up more than he'd meant to, Sam started to turn away and go back to his repairs. Rachel's voice at his back stopped him.

"Tell me about them, Sam. You've shown me pictures, but tell me what your children are like. I—I thought I'd get their rooms ready while you're gone. It might be hard for them coming into a strange place. They might be scared or homesick at first. There should be something special here for each of them."

She was right. Of course, she was right, and Sam understood once again why he had chosen Rachel. She had a way of anticipating a child's feelings and reactions that many adults had somehow lost over the years. It was almost a shame that she didn't have kids of her own. She should have them. From what Hal had said, it was a wonder she didn't, given all the guys panting around her. Sam frowned, then kicked that thought away. Rachel's personal life was none of his business. Besides, she was waiting....

Shrugging, Sam struggled to find the words that would describe his children and found that it was impossible. "I don't know," he said finally. "Janey...she's this chubby little butterball who waddles around the house. Her chief interest is still her toes and how many of them she can cram into her mouth. She loves to be tickled and cuddled, and she has this ratty pink teddy bear she calls 'Baby.' She never lets Zach out of her sight. And Zach, he's like a little cannonball, rushing everywhere, never slowing down. He's hot into the topic of dogs, 'woofs' as he calls them, and he's extremely protective of Janey. That doesn't mean they don't fight all the time. They do. Take one of Janey's toys and she'll beat you with her teddy bear until you let go. Zach steals her things on a regular basis just to rile her, I think. They love to sing with the radio. Loud. Really loud... and off-key." Sam had to smile, remembering his two budding performers.

He looked up to see that Rachel was smiling back at him. "And Annie?" she asked. "What does she like to do?"

Annie was harder. Annie was painful to talk about. "She's the mother of the world. Six years old and she'll adopt every injured animal, every broken doll, she'll bring any child that gets hurt to our house to bandage them up. Annie has a real need to take care of people. She's always been like that, but she used to enjoy other things, too, like riding her bike or playing dress up... or even digging in the dirt...." Sam's voice trailed off, not wanting to remember the reason for the changes in Annie.

"Well, you've certainly got plenty of dirt for your kids to play in here, Sam," Rachel said, motioning out the window to the unkempt yard. "They can dig to their hearts' content, maybe start a garden."

"Is that how you got so interested in flowers?" he asked suddenly. "Did you have a garden as a kid?" Sam hadn't known Rachel until she was fifteen. He didn't know much of her, anyway, but he did remember vague things. She hadn't had much, her clothes had not been well made, her mother had been forced to clean his parents' home to earn money. Still, she'd been a breath of air when they'd first met. She'd sparkled when she smiled and she'd smiled often. He suddenly wished he'd had more of a chance to get to know her, but—

"What was your life like as a child, Rachel?" he asked, surprising himself by voicing his thoughts.

He had apparently surprised *her,* too, stepped into forbidden territory. Her back stiffened, she lost her smile.

"I had a garden," she agreed, answering his earlier question. "You could do that easily. There's so much room here. The children could have a vegetable garden and try their hands at growing something. There are lots of things that aren't too hard to cultivate. Radishes grow fast, and even if kids don't like to eat them, it's still a rush to know that you've grown something that *someone* will eat. And there's plenty of room for more trees here, and lots of flower beds—" Rachel stopped talking.

"I'm sorry, this is your house," she said quietly. "I didn't mean to take over."

"Why not? You know that I want you to," he answered. Sam held her gaze with his own. "Why *are* you doing this, Rachel? Why are you helping me at all? It's clear that things haven't changed all that much between you and me. You haven't taken any money I've offered you, so why have you agreed to come here and help me at all? Why should *you* care about my children?"

Silence settled into the room; a long, uncomfortable silence.

"Kate," Rachel finally said, breaking into the stillness. "You're Kate's brother, your children are her nieces, her nephew. And Kate was always there for me. We were close."

She smiled a sudden and brilliant smile, tilting her chin up defiantly. "That's why I'm here, Sam."

So, Sam thought, his sister's friendship coupled with Rachel's soft spot for lonely kids was the *only* reason the lady was putting up with him at all. And he wanted her here just for his children's sake. If he was wise, he'd remember that. He wouldn't let himself forget that Rachel was simply his sister's friend and a potential source of quality child care. Any tender feelings he'd ever possessed had run out the door along with Donna. He certainly wasn't going to dredge them up again, not for anyone, especially not for a woman who *already* ran whenever he got too close.

The house was done, ready to be lived in . . . except for a few finishing touches, Rachel thought, letting herself in the front door.

In a basket on her arm were three sad-faced teddy bears, supersoft and guaranteed cuddly. Their pathetic little expressions looked sadder by the minute . . . as if they needed nurturing. As if they needed a child to give them a hug.

That was what she was hoping for as she placed each one on a bed upstairs. She wanted those kids to be so busy comforting their new furry friends that they wouldn't have time to think about the fact that they were starting a new life in a strange town. She just didn't want them to be scared or sad the first day in their new home.

Why are you doing this, Rachel? The question Sam had asked yesterday drifted into her consciousness. It was a good question, a tough one. She had no ready answers, even for herself. Rachel knew that what she had told Sam was only a half-truth. She was helping out partly because Sam and his children were related to her old friend, but even that wasn't enough. Kate had gotten her on the phone and attempted to persuade her to quit her job just the other night, but Rachel had resisted all Kate's efforts. Even friendship had its limits.

Still, she *was* helping him. How could she do otherwise when he was so concerned for his kids? That man loved his children and was worried for them. She couldn't just stand on the sidelines and do nothing at all. Neither, though, could she work here with him, not in his own home. That had become absolutely clear when she'd stood there in the prison of his arms. She had nearly died of desire and the need to hold herself distant. There was no way she wanted to live through such an experience again. At least, not with Sam.

The key turning in the lock brought Rachel out of her foggy attempts to understand and justify her motivations here. She hurried down the steps and arrived at the bottom just in time to see Sam coming in with two wiggly bundles in his arms. A little girl stood by his side, her serious little face turned toward Rachel.

Annie's pictures didn't do her justice. She was all dark curls and big blue eyes. She was Kate as Kate must have been as a child. Rachel couldn't have kept a smile from her face if she had fought with all her might.

"Annie," she said. "You have to be Annie. You're the image of pictures I've seen of your aunt Kate when she was your age."

Annie nodded solemnly at her. "I *am* Annie, and you are Rachel. Daddy said you couldn't stay, that we would have to make do with his cooking tonight. We are going to have hot dogs," she said, wrinkling her nose.

"Dogs. Woof." Rachel's attention was drawn away from Annie as Sam let Janey and Zach slide to the floor.

"Woof," Zach repeated.

Rachel managed not to laugh as Zach stood tall and Janey peeked out from behind him, smiling shyly. When Rachel smiled back, the little girl crept out. She held out her teddy bear.

"Baby," she said.

"Pleased to meet you, Baby," Rachel replied. "And you too, Janey and Zach. But I don't think you have to rely on your dad's cooking for tonight, anyway, Annie. I can stay that long at least. Your daddy has been driving for a while. He probably wants to settle down and visit with the three of you now. Time enough for him to start cooking tomorrow."

Sam was down on one knee pulling a handkerchief from his pocket to wipe away a smudge of dirt Zach was sporting on the end of his nose. At her words he turned swiftly, his gaze meeting her own. Her heart nearly forgot to beat when she stared into his deep blue eyes. He touched his fingers to his little boy's cheek.

"That's kind of you, Rachel. Thank you," he said. "We do need some time."

It was a simple statement, nothing extraordinary, but Rachel suddenly wondered what had happened in the last day or two. Sam looked tired and sad.

When he got up and started into the other room, Rachel noticed how Annie quickly grabbed his hand as if she was afraid he'd get away from her. Together the four of them shuffled at a slow pace into the living room. Sam sat down and Annie crawled up on his lap. Not Janey and Zach. They were off like a flash, looking for adventure.

Sam started to get up, taking Annie with him, but Rachel shook her head.

"Don't worry, Sam. They're just exploring. I'll make sure you don't end up with more purple-polka-dotted curtains," Rachel said, turning to follow the two little ones.

"No, no, I will do that," Annie said suddenly, jumping up. "*I* always watch Janey and Zach," the little girl said stubbornly. "Just don't go away, Daddy. Do not move," the yylittle girl ordered.

"Annie..." Sam said, reaching for her hand, but she was already two steps away.

"I'll be back," she promised. "Don't leave. Don't dare get up and leave, Daddy."

"Never again, Annie. Not ever. You understand?"

She nodded solemnly, but still she was dancing nervously from foot to foot. Her eyes were darting around as if she was unsure what to do.

When she had left the room completely, Sam pushed a restless hand back through his thick, black hair. He let out a deep breath.

"She missed you," Rachel said by way of explanation. "It's natural that she wouldn't want to leave your side."

Sam turned dark blue eyes on Rachel. "She had nightmares every day, Mrs. Nelson said. I can't believe I did that to my child."

Rachel sucked in a breath. "Sam," she said slowly. "Don't blame yourself. She'll learn that you won't leave her, that you'd never hurt her."

"You're damn right about that," Sam agreed, pinning Rachel where she stood with the fierceness of his gaze. "I'd never do anything that would hurt her, not if I could help it. My children will always be first with me, above all else."

Rachel had no doubts about that as she watched Annie leading the twins back into the room. They had found their teddy bears and the other toys that had been left upstairs, too. Sam studied them closely and she could see the love and pride written on his face. Restlessly he smoothed his hand over Annie's curls as the little girl finally relaxed and began to talk about what they would do the next day.

Quietly Rachel slipped from the room and moved into the kitchen to make dinner. She was in the middle of rolling pizza dough when she looked up to find four brown eyes peeping up at her over the rim of the table.

"Want to help?" she asked with a grin.

Janey and Zach nodded, their heads bobbing up and down.

Smiling, Rachel set them up at the end of the table with their own bit of dough. She spread sauce and cheese on the main course as the two little munchkins rolled their dough into snakes, then pounded them flat, laughing, inordinately pleased with themselves.

She was just putting the first pizza in the oven when Annie came in. "Janey, Zach," the little girl said, her hands on her hips. "You must not be in here."

"It's okay, Annie, they're fine. Do you think you could help me, too?" Rachel motioned to the remaining half of the dough and the other supplies on the table. She picked up an apron and held it out.

Annie looked longingly at her brother and sister stringing out the dough, then she glanced back over her shoulder, fear in her eyes. "I have to watch Daddy," she explained in a small voice.

Rachel shook her head. "Your daddy's sleeping, Annie. I can see him from here."

"But if I look away—"

"He'll still be sleeping. He isn't going anywhere. Nowhere at all."

Reluctantly Annie agreed to be helped into the apron. She pinched and patted the dough. She took the rolling pin and madc long strokes back and forth, pushing the dough into a lopsided circle, but Rachel couldn't keep from noticing that not a minute went by when Annie didn't glance into the next room to see if Sam was still there. This was a child who needed help.

The thought wouldn't go away. It was still bothering her two hours later when Rachel stood before a still sleepy Sam at the door. He had dark shadows of stubble on his cheeks, his shirt was open, and his dark hair was tousled from where he'd tossed and turned on the couch. He hadn't slept well. She doubted the night would bring him any more rest, judging from the anxious way Annie was watching him.

"Thank you, Rachel," he said in a sleep-roughened voice. He reached out and raked the backs of two fingers across her cheek and she couldn't have stepped away if she'd tried.

She couldn't even breathe in. "You're a stubborn, hard-headed woman, but a good one. A very good one."

"Take care, Sam," she whispered, knowing she wouldn't be coming back to this house again. "Goodbye, Annie. Kiss Janey and Zach for me. I'll see you around town."

"Thank you for the pizza, Rachel. You cook better than Mrs. Nelson," Annie said solemnly, and Rachel knew she'd been granted the highest compliment.

But as she walked away and heard the door close behind her, she wondered how they were going to get along without someone to take care of them—and how was Sam going to go back to work when Annie couldn't bear to have him out of her sight? She hoped he'd be able to find a housekeeper soon.

The ride home was quiet, too quiet after the babbling of the twins all evening. Rachel didn't want quiet, she didn't want to think... or remember that little girl's sad and wistful look.

She closed her mind to her thoughts, to Sam and his babies. When she got home, she shut her door behind her and flipped on the television set, even though she had no interest whatsoever in watching television.

Sitting there, willing herself not to think about that family across town, Rachel was grateful when the doorbell rang—and surprised. It was already getting late. Who'd be coming to visit her now?

Opening the door, she met the smile of Cynthia Watts.

"That man—" Cynthia began, holding out a thin florist's package. "He's something. But then I guess I can't complain. I'm the one who let him talk me into making a delivery at this time of night. Hope you like it."

Blinking, Rachel thanked her friend, then took the package inside. She peeled back the wrapping. Inside was a single white rose, wreathed by baby's breath. Who would wake Cynthia to send flowers at this time of night? Silly question. Who was the only man who had ever given her flowers at all?

Rachel gently touched the petals, found the card.

"This one's not a bribe, Rachel. I just wanted to say thank you. Thank you so much for everything. You're one very special lady. Sam."

Swallowing, Rachel wanted to scream. She felt the lump forming in her throat and the dampness at the backs of her eyes. *Not a bribe.* Damn the man. This was more of a bribe than anything else had been. He *knew* she'd just come from his house. He *knew* she'd been unable to resist his children and that she couldn't help wanting to comfort that lonely and scared little girl. He knew that telling her she was special would make her feel like a total jerk turning away from those helpless babies. Oh yes, Sam Grayson, this beautiful, lone blossom was most definitely a bribe. Hadn't the man indicated that he would do anything for his children? Hadn't he sworn he would always put them first?

And as Rachel placed the rose in a bud vase and tucked herself into bed she damned the man again. Sleep wasn't going to come easily for *her* this night, either, it seemed.

All night she tossed in her bed. She didn't want to give in, she certainly didn't want to spend more time with Sam. If only—if only she could convince herself that it was really okay to walk away from Sam's wide-eyed little waifs. If she was already committed to something truly important, if she'd learned to love Don, if she could find the sparkle in her heart when he was around, things would be different. She'd have her own family to care for, she could walk away guilt free. But she'd sent Don away. And while he'd elected to come back, to see how she felt after the death of her mother was well behind her and her emotions had mended, he wasn't here now. She didn't know if time had worked some magic.

And in the morning, nothing had changed. Bob Engalls still hadn't turned into her knight in shining armor. Don was still away. She couldn't summon him and offer him hope that might not be justified. And there were still children across town who needed her help.

Rachel dressed quickly, she called in a temporary office worker for Hal so that he would have someone to do her job while he looked for someone more permanent. She took a deep breath and closed the door to her house.

In fifteen minutes she was at Sam's door.

When he opened it and stood there towering over her, he looked much the same as last night, just a little more rough around the edges. He wasn't wearing a shirt this time, and the top button of his jeans was undone. He was as sexy as a man could be without setting everything around him on fire. Rachel could barely open her mouth... but she did.

"All right, you win, Sam Grayson. You win," she said, holding out the white rose. "But just remember that I'm stubborn and I'm hardheaded and you and I don't get along. Don't forget that."

"I never have, Rachel. Not ever," he said in an early-morning rasp. He reached out to pull her inside, and his fingers sliding against her bare arm sent a ripple of tension and need throughout her body. Rachel's stomach began to flutter.

"This might not work, Sam," she whispered urgently. He was still touching her, it was all she could do to keep from pressing her free hand to his chest to push herself away...but she was afraid that resting her fingers on his warm, naked skin would be the biggest mistake she would ever make. "You and I—we might not be able to get along together."

"We might not. I know, Rachel. We'll see," he whispered back, dragging his fingers slowly away from her. "Come inside," he urged. "Come here and we'll see if we can work things out, if we can work together with no regrets."

But Sam's voice sounded almost as uncertain as she felt, and Rachel knew that what Sam was asking was impossible. She was going to regret this decision many times over. She was going to be sorry she had ever made a commitment to Sam and his children. Especially when Sam was a man with nothing to offer her but money... and the promise of a great many sleepless nights.

Chapter Four

When Rachel fished out the key to Sam's door the next morning and let herself in, he was in the kitchen trying to dress Zach while Janey climbed on his back. Zach twisted from side to side, making the whole process that much more difficult.

"You little squirt. Stay still." Sam chuckled as Zach giggled back. "No piggyback rides now, Janey," he managed as his daughter got a choke hold on him and dug her chubby little toes into his spinal column.

"Up," Janey insisted, hanging on tighter.

Rachel stood there surveying the scene, Annie sitting quietly at the table drawing a picture while Sam wrestled with the babies. Her heart gave an unwelcome lurch, testimony to the doubts that continued to assail her. Still, she couldn't help smiling at the trio rolling around on the floor. Annie, in contrast, looked like the only adult in the group.

"Annie, what a wonderful picture of a castle. It looks like you've had a lot of practice drawing," she said quietly as the little girl looked up and nodded hello before continuing with her task.

Sam stopped dead still at the sound of Rachel's voice and jerked up his head. He obviously hadn't even known that she'd entered the house. His hair was mussed, his shirt collar was crooked from Janey's tugging, his white shirtsleeves were rolled up. A tiny sock dangled from his fingers.

"*You're* early," he admonished softly.

"And *you* agreed that it was my job to get the kids dressed in the morning. Didn't we spend all of yesterday establishing what my responsibilities would be?" she asked, shaking her head and smiling down at him. "Hey, Zach, let's get those clothes on, tiger," she said, sinking down cross-legged on the floor and holding her hands out to the little boy. "Then we can get right to the good stuff—food and toys."

Zach smiled broadly. He rolled onto his tummy and struggled to his feet, one sock on and one sock off, tumbling toward Rachel.

"Toss me those overalls, all right, Sam?" she said.

Sam sat up. He slid Janey around till she was resting against his hip and raked one hand back through his hair to straighten it. "It's your first day on the job, Rachel. There's no point in overdoing it right away. I was *supposed* to have everything rolling along before you got here." He pasted a stern look on his face and left the overalls lying on the floor.

Janey grabbed a bit of his hair and tried to shove it in her mouth. Rachel wasn't sure how, but Sam managed not to laugh. He continued to give *her* that disappointed parent look.

Catching Zach up in her arms when he teetered close, Rachel rolled her eyes at Sam. "Sam, I'm sorry I spoiled your plans, and that's very generous of you to want to make things easy for me my first day, but I grew up with four younger brothers and sisters, in case you've forgotten. I think I can manage the snaps and buckles on a pair of overalls. Now give me those clothes so I can get everyone fed and you can get off to work. By now Hal's probably driving the temp insane by messing around with the accounting figures. You'll need to get down there and soothe everyone's ruffled feathers."

A small silence ensued, then Sam shrugged, climbing to his feet.

"All right, I'm off, but if you need me you've got the number. Don't overdo things, I don't expect you to become a slave, I can handle the tougher stuff once I get home and—"

"Sam."

He leaned down toward her. She snapped Zach's overalls and dropped a kiss on the little boy's hair before standing him on his feet. Then she turned to Janey who was shifting from one foot to the other, struggling to get close enough for her own kiss.

"What, Rachel?"

"I don't blow away every time the wind whistles, Sam. And I'm not a teenage girl anymore. When I say I'll do something, I follow through, whether we're talking about dancing, working, or spending my days with three adorable children. You can count on that. You don't have to coddle me, or worry. Now, do you think I can get these babies fed, Sam... or do you have any more instructions you need to give me?"

Sam looked down at Rachel and at Janey. His younger daughter now had her palms on the floor, her little bottom in the air as she peeped through her legs at the world turned upside down. "Just one," he replied, clearing his throat and raising one brow as he gave Rachel an apologetic smile that sent her heart into a faster rhythm. "The diapers—they're in the front closet."

Laughing, Rachel rose to her feet and picked up Janey. "Come on, munchkin, say goodbye to your daddy and let's go get you dry."

It took a few minutes, but finally Sam had kissed all his children, hugged them twice and stepped to the door.

"Thank you, Rachel," he said, pausing in a stream of sunlight that filtered into the big kitchen.

Rachel sucked in air. Even though the sunlight killed her ability to make out his features, she could still see the silhouette of a long, tall man. She still felt that husky voice resonate throughout her body. Sam's gentle words and concern struck a chord deep within Rachel, and she found herself wondering what it would be like to push close to him the way Janey had done. She hoped he couldn't see the telltale signs of heat that crept up her face at the thought.

"We'll see you at the end of the day, Sam. Don't worry," she said as calmly as she could. Carefully she closed the door, not waiting for him to do so.

Sam was gone now. She could breathe—and survive the rest of the day.

Turning away from the door, Rachel proceeded to do what she'd spent a lifetime doing. She cared for the children in her charge—and she pushed Sam as far back in her thoughts as he would go.

She made pancakes and topped them with cherry eyes and a pineapple smile. She sang songs and built houses out of blocks, she changed diapers and wiped sticky fingers. She played finger games, and with the exception of hand washing, Janey and Zach seemed completely delighted with this new lady who'd infiltrated their home.

Annie, however, was another story.

The little girl who'd enjoyed pizza the night before, now sat silent and rigid. She shook her head when Rachel invited her to join in a game. She turned toward the window every few minutes.

"It's too bad that school let out for the summer last week. You could have met some other kids," Rachel said. "But once you've had a day or two to get your bearings, we'll round some people up and invite them over. I know most of the kids in this town. Would that be all right?"

Annie took a tiny nibble of the macaroni and cheese Rachel had made for lunch. "I guess so, thank you," she said in a tiny little voice that barely carried across the kitchen.

More silence.

Annie shifted on her chair. She looked out the window again.

Rachel managed not to sigh. She thought a minute, then sank down on her knees next to the little girl's chair. "Annie, your daddy might be having lunch right now. Would you like to call the lumberyard just to say hello?"

It was as if a small candle lit up behind Annie's eyes. She pressed her hands together and looked up at Rachel. "Yes, please. Could I talk to Daddy just for a moment, do you think? He might need me for something."

Smiling her agreement, Rachel picked up the phone and punched in the numbers. She handed the receiver to Annie, then moved away to give the child some privacy.

It was such a small thing, letting her call her dad, but it seemed to make a difference. Rachel could see Annie's hands fluttering around excitedly out of the corner of her eye. She could hear the animation in her voice.

The terror and heartbreak that child must have endured when she'd realized that her mother had walked away from home—Rachel knew she couldn't even begin to imagine it. Like the twins, *she'd* been younger when her own father had left. Her pain had been real when she'd finally realized she'd been abandoned, but it had come after the fact, when she could no longer even remember the man who'd fathered her. She hadn't gone to bed happy and awakened to find her world dissolving. Not like Annie.

"He was very happy to hear from me," Annie said when she hung up. "Daddy misses me when he's away." The girl's eager little face, her eyes that were suddenly shining, had Rachel blinking to see through the mist that drifted across her eyes.

No wonder Sam was so concerned and had worked so hard to lure her away from the lumberyard. Watching Annie now, feeling her own heart break for this child who'd had the magic snatched from her life, Rachel knew what Sam must have suspected. Having witnessed firsthand this little girl's grief, she *had* to do whatever was possible to turn that sadness to smiles. It was just the way things were and always had been with her. She couldn't ignore a child in need.

She couldn't ignore Sam, either. Frowning, Rachel shoved that nasty little suspicion to the back of her mind. It wasn't true, of course. She had walked away from the man many times. But he had never pursued her in the past. He had never had a reason to do so before. Now he did. Now he needed her—for his children's sake. And she had darn well better remember that that was the only reason she was here. He'd sworn off love. She couldn't blame him. He'd found a goodbye note in the dark and had been left to raise his children alone.

And she had a job to do, that was all. Once she'd helped Annie and the twins to resume normal, healthy lives, her task would be over. She'd be a small speck of history to the Graysons. Until then, all of her attention, every scrap, had to be centered on this woeful little girl dangling her legs from the kitchen chair and on those two sweet babies upstairs. Not because she'd been hired to do so, but because her heart would let her do no less.

"You didn't have any dessert," she said gently, smiling at Annie who was still glowing a bit. "Do you think you might find a place to fit a scoop of chocolate ice cream now? I'm sure I saw a bowl of ice cream in the freezer that told me it belonged to Annie Grayson. Let's peek inside the freezer and see if it's still there."

Other children might have giggled. Other children might have rolled their eyes and said, "Oh, Rachel, don't be silly."

Annie didn't giggle or roll her eyes. She looked up at Rachel, studying her. Then, "I think I might like to have a bowl of ice cream now, thank you," she said as she seated herself obediently at the table. "Daddy said he will be home very soon. Just a few more hours."

A sigh simmered deep within Rachel's consciousness. This little girl needed so much. So very much. But Annie wouldn't recover what she had lost in a single day. And as the little girl had indicated, this day was almost gone. Sam would be here in a few hours. With his let's-make-love voice, his bedroom blue eyes.

A churning began deep within Rachel. She watched as Annie finished her ice cream and then quietly carried her dishes to the sink, standing on tiptoe to carefully place them down into the basin.

"Maybe you'd like to help me make dinner for your daddy again. Do you think he'd like that?" she asked.

Annie looked back over her shoulder and nodded. "Yes, please."

Rachel wondered what it would be like to hear Annie laugh or to see her get so excited that she forgot to be polite. She wondered what the sound of Annie and Sam's laughter joining together would sound like—and found she wanted to know.

"I know what we'll do," she said to Annie. "Let's see if there's a cookbook around here. You pick something out while I go wake up your brother and sister. Then we'll come back in here and make an incredible, wonderful mess. How about it?"

Annie opened her mouth and Rachel knew that the child was going to volunteer to get the twins out of bed herself. Quickly Rachel shook her head.

"I don't have a clue as to what your dad would like, and I really do need your help, Annie," she said. "Maybe something for dessert. You know him better than I do. You'll be able to find something special."

Rachel was pretty sure she looked calm on the outside, but as she located a cookbook for Annie and went to get the twins up from their nap, she couldn't keep from looking at the clock eating up the minutes.

Time *was* passing. Sam *would* be here shortly. Surely this wasn't anticipation she was feeling. Of course not. She focused on the weekend ahead, concentrated on making plans, charting out a day with some friends.

Then, coming into the twins' bedroom, Rachel shunted even those thoughts away. She picked up a sleepy-eyed, yawning Janey and smiled, hugging her close.

"Come on, buttercup. Time to rise and count your toes."

Janey managed a sleepy giggle. Zach rolled over, his hair sticking up at all angles. He promptly reached down and grasped his foot, bringing it close to his face.

"Toes," he declared proudly. "Dee?"

"Your daddy's not home yet, Zach," she told him. *But of course, he will be. Soon,* Rachel admitted, finally acknowledging what had been bothering her all afternoon. The fact was that she could face these little darlings all day, every day, and was glad to do so. She would willingly stay with them long enough to help, without letting them become too dependent on her. But she had to admit that the thought of being near their father was a totally different proposition, one she had to deal with. Now.

Sam had blown back into her life like an unsettling wind, knocking her off course. The fact that this strong man had faced so much, that his ego had been torn and he'd come back fighting, earned him her reluctant admiration. But his willingness to sacrifice his pride and crawl on his knees to a woman who had once scorned him, and all for the sake of his children, *that* kicked her straight in the heart. And she had yet to adjust, to right herself and find her way back to her own path.

But she would. She definitely would—had to.

She'd grown up, away from Sam. There were other men in her life now. And love *could* grow out of something like her friendship with Don. It didn't have to start out as this devastating flame and frost that had always colored her relationship with Sam. She didn't have to let herself be pulled in by those sensations this time.

Sam was her employer. No more. Their paths were different—separate.

There. Rachel moved into the kitchen with the kids and gave the twins a set of spoons to play with. By the time she and Annie had taken the cake out of the oven, Rachel had decided that this situation *could* work. Sam was her employer. That was all. All she had to do was follow the basic rules of business.

But when the doorbell rang a bit later and she faced the messenger bearing a bouquet of larkspur and Queen Anne's lace, Rachel realized that the basic rules of business just didn't apply to her and Sam.

She was still foolish enough to feel touched by his gift. He was still uncertain that he could count on her to stay. Rachel wished she could reassure him in some way, but to do that she would have to get close to Sam—and that just wasn't going to happen. Not in this lifetime.

The house was just ahead. Sam could feel himself tightening up as he got closer, wanting to rush. A vision of Rachel waiting on the porch, a baby on either hip and Annie at her side, pushed into his consciousness.

"Hell," Sam said, forcing the thought aside as he made himself slow down. The woman had only been at his house a few hours and already he was casting her in a role she wasn't meant to play. A role he wouldn't *want* her to play, he reminded himself.

If he was eager to get home, it was only because he'd missed his children. The bride of Frankenstein could have been caring for them and he'd be just as eager to get there. Heck, in that case, he'd have been there hours ago rescuing them, Sam thought with a smile.

And Rachel was just his employee. He paid her to be there, and he had darn well better remember that and keep his ludicrous daydreams in check.

But when he arrived, reality wasn't as far off base from his vision as he would have expected. Annie *was* on the porch waiting, and Rachel was hot on the trail of Zach who had wriggled out through the half-open door. Janey had a death grip on the tail of Rachel's blouse which had come untucked.

Rachel was hauling Zach up into her arms and grasping Janey's hand at the same time, just as Sam stepped up onto the porch.

"Nice day?" he drawled, looking at the way Rachel's hair had come loose from the ribbon that was tying it back.

She blew out hard, sending a loose lock hanging over her forehead to fly up in the air and descend—right where it had been resting before. Her jeans had a rip in the knee where one hadn't been that morning, her white blouse had lost a button and sported tiny fingerprints of various colors near the waist. But standing there barefoot, holding on to his children, she was more beautiful than Sam had ever seen her.

"Nice day," she said, following his perusal of her with her own eyes. "We were painting," she explained.

"Hor-ey," Janey added, looking at Rachel.

Rachel looked down at the hole in the knee of her pants and blank spot where her button had been. "A lame horse," she agreed with a smile and a shrug. "What can I say?"

She didn't have to say anything. It was clear that his babies had enjoyed themselves and that Rachel, while she looked disheveled, seemed undaunted and unfrazzled by her day.

It was only when he moved to take Zach from her arms, and his own hand barely brushed her arm, that she jerked back. But not soon enough for him. He had felt her warmth. He could see the way her breathing had kicked up faster. So this was going to be awkward every day, was it? This meeting over and over?

"I'll repay you for your losses," he said gruffly, indicating her jeans with a wave of his hand.

Rachel shook her head violently. "Hey, I'm a big girl, Sam. I make my own choices. If I end up with a rip here and there, it's my own responsibility." He started to open his mouth again, but she shook her head.

"Dinner will be ready in two minutes," she said, turning back toward the door. "Annie helped make it."

Annie, who had been hovering at his side the whole time, nodded at Rachel's words. "No rutabagas, Daddy," she announced. "I made a cake."

She was sticking closer to him than most children would, but then what had he expected? She'd only been here two days, she hadn't had time to even begin to adjust. But Rachel had been sensitive to her needs today. She'd let his child call him at work, she'd paid attention to the panic signals his daughter was sending, and she hadn't berated Annie for her fears. It would take time, but he had every hope that Rachel would finally breathe contentment back into his child. For that he owed the lady big-time. By the time Annie was on the road back to normal, Sam wondered how deep his indebtedness and his gratitude would go. He wondered if every day when he came home, Rachel was going to send a shot of whiskey-hot desire coursing through his veins. Hell, he hoped not.

Following Rachel inside, he looked around the kitchen. It was ten times more spotless than he had left it this morning. There was a tablecloth on the table, an aroma in the air that made him realize he really was ravenous and Rachel bustling about the kitchen as though she belonged here.

But of course she didn't. Even now she was moving back toward the door.

"Eat?" Zach said to Rachel.

She shook her head, placing one hand on the door frame as she turned. "No, Zach, I have to go home for now. I'll see you in the morning, Sam." Her voice was soft, her eyes uncertain. Quickly she bent down, giving the twins the hugs they wanted and smiling at Annie.

"You made a fine cake," she said gently. "Your daddy will be proud."

And then she was gone, like a wisp of wind that came through and disappeared so fast you wondered if it had even happened.

"I'll be right back, Annie. Keep your eye on Janey and Zach, all right? We'll eat in just a minute."

Pushing out the door, he called to Rachel just as she was stepping down off the porch.

"Let me walk you to your car," he said.

Rachel turned, and Sam stood above her on the porch, looking down into her upturned face. She bit her lip, and he could see that she didn't really want him there with her.

Still, she nodded, and Sam fell into step beside her. He breathed in the scent of her, soap and baby powder and woman. It curled around him, making him aware of her nearness. Glancing to the side, he couldn't help but notice the gap in her blouse where the button was missing, or ignore the satin spot of vulnerable skin exposed to his gaze.

"Thank you—for the flowers, Sam. You really don't need to do that anymore, though, you know. I don't run out on my employers without proper notice."

So she thought he was still trying to bribe her. Well—why *was* he still sending her flowers? Maybe because they suited her, because she liked them so much, because she was right and he *did* want something from her? Sam nipped that thought in the bud. Darn it, what difference did it make why he was sending the damn flowers, anyway? He just was.

When a man sent a woman flowers on a regular basis, it usually meant something. The thought fluttered in like a red flag. He grimaced. His circumstances couldn't be called usual, but still...

Stopping by the car, he tried to turn his thoughts from the direction they were headed. "You need a new blouse," he chastised, the words slipping gruffly from his lips.

Instantly she looked down and slid her palm over the skin already turning a pale pink.

"Because of this?" She managed a laugh even though her skin was rosy. "All I need is a button and a needle and thread. This blouse is fine."

Sam frowned down at the garment in question, at the slender hand holding the edges in place.

"It's got paint on it, and heaven knows what else. Those little boogers of mine really took advantage of you, didn't they?"

Rachel stuck her chin in the air. "They did not. They're absolute little sweethearts, and I encouraged them to be messy and noisy and to play their hearts out."

Rocking back on his heels, Sam leveled his gaze at her and grinned. "Rachel Allyn, are you spoiling my children?"

She tucked her hands into her hip pockets and leaned forward, looking directly at him. Her left brow was raised in a challenge.

"I made them eat peas with their lunch," she announced sternly.

"Well, then," he drawled. "I guess that shoots the spoiling theory to pieces. I hate peas."

"You wouldn't. Not the way I make them."

A low chuckle escaped Sam. "Rachel, I'm not an eighteen-month-old kid, I'll beg you to remember. And you're never going to talk *me* into eating peas."

She shrugged, the lift of her shoulders almost spreading her blouse again. "You're worse than any child I've ever met, Sam."

Sam managed to keep his eyes off her chest, but just barely. And it was obvious that Rachel could tell which way his thoughts had turned.

She pulled her hands from her pockets and crossed them over her chest. "I want to thank you—for not making a stink because Annie called you at work."

"Make a stink? Rachel, Annie's my child. I'm just glad that you suggested that she call. She can call—*you* can call anytime it's necessary."

Rachel tilted her head to the side. "Yes, well, I'm just glad that it consoled her a bit. She seemed a little brighter afterward. I thought you'd want to know that her day wasn't completely awful."

Concern resonated in her voice. Sam felt gratitude growing like a flower deep within him. Thank goodness Rachel had come to him. He raised one hand, nearly touched her cheek, then stopped.

"I already knew that, Rachel. I did. This is the first day in a long string of days that I haven't worried about my children. I knew you'd do whatever it took to get them through without me. I trust you with my babies. That's what I've been trying to tell you all along. I know you'll look out for them come what may. And I'm incredibly thankful."

He took one step closer, placed his hands on the shining red roof of her car, framing her body with his own. She tilted her head back farther, accommodating his height as she leaned back against the door of the car.

"I didn't do anything special."

But Sam knew that was wrong. Unable to stop himself, he reached out and touched a bright strand of her hair. Lightly, gently, he let the dark web of silk slide against his palm. The warmth of her breath caressed the back of his hand and sent sudden heat coursing through his blood.

"You *did* do something special, Rachel. You're here." And sliding his hand up, he threaded his fingers through her hair, pulling her closer. He tilted his head and brought his mouth down to cover hers.

She was warm cream, soft, the petals of her lips feeding him. With a groan, Sam dragged her closer. He felt her slender hands crawl to his shoulders and he was lost.

Her heartbeat became his, he wanted to wrap her up inside himself and hold her there. He wanted to peel that plain white cotton blouse off her shoulders and trail his lips down the length of her body.

Rachel shifted against him, her legs moved against his. He licked at her lips, slid his wide palms down her back and over the softness of curves that filled his hand.

"Sam," she said as he kissed his way across the silk of her cheek, nipping at the sensitive flesh beneath her ear.

Her shiver fired him, and he started to lift her higher against him. Her hands fluttering against his chest made him wild with want.

"Sam, no." He froze, realizing that she was pushing against him, not pulling him closer.

Harsh reality sizzled through the sky like lightning. He'd nearly been on top of her, ready to take her, with his children in the house behind him and the woman herself struggling against him.

Pushing away, he stepped back, leaving her standing there, bracing herself against the car.

He could almost see her pulling herself together. The deep breaths, the shaky hands. When she managed a tremulous smile, he cursed himself. What did he expect? Twice in his life he'd managed to read a woman wrong in a major way: once, years ago, when he'd thought he and Rachel were becoming friends, and then again, when he'd read love in Donna's eyes where there'd been none. But this time—this time, there was no question of reading the woman wrong. She was his employee, for God's sake. And a reluctant employee, at that. He'd practically dragged her from her old job and into this new one. He had no business pushing this kind of intimacy on her.

"I—I'm sorry, Sam, I just—" She held her hands out, palms up, searching for words as she attempted to make light of the fact that he'd been all over her a moment ago.

Sam swung around, holding up one hand. "*You're* sorry? When we both know this was my fault. I'm the one to apologize. This was—a mistake. A big mistake. But you don't have to worry. I won't let my appreciation get the best of me again."

He watched as Rachel collected the remaining tattered strands of her dignity and wrapped herself in them. She opened her eyes wide and stared at him dead-on, even though her cheeks were flushed with rose.

"I was apologizing, Sam, because we both know that I wasn't exactly a passive participant in that kiss. But—you're right. It *was* a big mistake. If you want to express your appreciation, I think the flowers will do. They *are* beautiful."

"And not nearly as overwhelming as a man bending you back over his arm, I'd guess," he said, still kicking at himself.

So she took the flowers as a gesture of thanks, did she? Well, good, because that was a better reason than he could come up with. He certainly hadn't sent them because their softness reminded him of her. Or because he couldn't stop thinking of lying down with her on a bed of grass and crimson flowers.

Damn.

"I didn't mean to spoil your first day on the job, Rachel," he said quietly.

"Me, either," she agreed. "So maybe we should both just forget this ever happened."

He nodded, opening the door of her car for her as she climbed inside. "It never *should* have happened. We'll forget it completely," he said.

Like hell, Rachel Allyn, he thought as she drove away in her little red car. If she thought he was ever going to forget the feel of her body locked to his, or the passion that had gotten him in its grip, then she must have a pretty high opinion of his self-control.

And Sam knew for a fact that Rachel had never had a high opinion of him at all.

Chapter Five

The road was a strip of black charcoal Rachel tried to burn up beneath her wheels, as she raced on in an attempt to avoid her thoughts. If she could just get far enough away, if she could just move fast enough, then she'd be able to forget that she'd been kissing Sam Grayson just a few moments ago.

She would forget that it had been wonderful. Heady. She could hide from the fact that she wanted more.

That did it. Rachel hit the main part of town and pulled over into the grocery store parking lot. She needed normal. She needed sane. She needed safe everyday activity.

Climbing from the car and rounding up a grocery cart, she pushed her way mindlessly to the store. Her lips were still tingling, her body was still throbbing. How could she have done what she'd done?

Only a short time ago she'd been calmly reflecting on the fact that she needed to be careful not to let the children become too dependent on her. Now it appeared that *she* was the one who needed watching.

Rachel tossed groceries into her cart, paying little attention to what she was doing.

How could she have followed Sam's lead so easily? And she couldn't even blame the man, damn him. Sam had been going through a lot, he'd been betrayed by his wife, he was half-crazed with worry about his kids. It was only natural that all that pent-up emotion would explode sometime, someway.

A picture of herself with her arms fastened around Sam's neck flickered into Rachel's mind, and she swung around the corner recklessly, nearly knocking over a display of canned goods.

She should have stopped things sooner—but she hadn't. She almost hadn't been able to find the words to call a halt at all. Only a distant memory of dancing in Sam's arms while he married another woman had brought her to her senses. Because the truth was that right now Sam was just as wounded as his kids. In time, he'd heal. And in spite of his protests to the contrary, he might even marry again. He was, after all, a healthy male. He would need a woman, and in time, he'd see the benefits of marriage both for him and for his children. Like Annie, the change wouldn't take place overnight, but it would happen. And when it did—when it did—

Rachel gave up all pretense of shopping. She pushed her cart blindly toward the registers, not wanting to finish her thoughts.

They barged in, anyway. When Sam finally went looking for a wife, the past was going to repeat itself. She would once again watch Sam dance away with another woman.

Rachel stopped dead in her tracks. She looked down in her cart at the three dozen cans of green beans and ten heads of lettuce. The man was clearly turning her into a brainless twit.

"Get a grip, Rachel," she muttered to herself. So what if Sam had broken her heart when she was just fifteen by telling his Donna that Rachel Allyn was poor and poverty-stricken and needed help, not gossip? So what if she'd made the mistake of losing herself in Sam's arms tonight?

After all, she was *not* fifteen anymore, and she certainly was just as normal and just as healthy as Sam. There was no point in beating up on herself because she'd enjoyed his kisses. What woman wouldn't?

None of this was going to matter in the long run. Sam was going to remarry; and she was going to walk down the aisle wearing a white dress and a glowing smile herself. Someday they'd both probably look back on this day with a little amazement and a lot of laughs at how carried away they'd been.

Someday she'd feel that same fire and flame in the arms of her husband. So this day didn't matter, not at all.

"Hey, Rachel." The cashier stared at her cart as she rolled up next to the register. "Looks like you're planning on eating a lot of salad."

Rachel looked down at her pitiful, ridiculous collection of groceries and shook her head at her own foolishness. She found a grin somewhere and lifted one shoulder in a shrug. "I'm planning a lot of things, Pete," she agreed, fishing out her cash.

And not one of them involved Sam Grayson.

Several days later Rachel joined Annie in the kitchen just after the twins had gone down for their midday snooze. The little girl was once again drawing. It had been her main occupation for the past few days.

"Maybe we could frame some of your pictures and hang them up, Annie. Would you like that?"

The little girl bunched her shoulders. She went on with her drawing. "Mommy's—my mother's pictures were hanging in our house," she finally said. "Mine are not good enough."

Her words were like a blow to Rachel. She knew without question that someone else had once made that same statement to Annie. And there was no way in heaven that Sam would ever have hurt his little girl that way.

"*I* like your pictures," Rachel said, even though she knew that her opinion was not one that would count in this instance.

For two seconds Annie turned to her, a slight spark of hope shining from the depths of her eyes. Then she took a deep breath, the light dimming. She turned back to her paper, stared long and hard at the crayon in her hand, as though it were some dreaded enemy.

"If I keep trying," she said finally, squaring her small shoulders and turning back to her picture, "I might get better."

And your mother might love you; she might come back. Rachel didn't need to hear the words to know what Annie was thinking.

This little girl looked so stoic, her shoulders pushed back bravely, her lips firm and determined, but inside, oh, inside, Rachel knew what she was feeling, what she was thinking. She knew about trying to win love that seemed unwinnable. What she didn't know was how to help this child. She wasn't sure if there was any way at all to open the door to Annie's heart and heal her hurt, when the little girl was riding down the wrong road all the way.

Rachel didn't know much about Donna Grayson, either, but she'd bet her soul that sweet Annie could draw a million pictures, she could bleed right onto the paper and spill her heart out in a masterpiece that rivaled any of the world's great artists...and it wouldn't bring her mother back. At least it wouldn't give Annie what she was looking for.

Running on instinct and instinct alone, Rachel sank down onto the chair next to Annie. She slid her hand across the table, into the little girl's line of vision. Close enough not to be ignored, but not near enough to startle.

She didn't know what to say. She knew she had to say something.

"My father was a great baseball fan," Rachel said softly. "After he left home, I played on a local team for years, hoping he'd read about me in the papers, that he'd be proud of me."

Silence.

So much silence. She shouldn't have spoken, Rachel thought. It was an intrusion into Annie's pain, it was presumptuous. Letting that little girl know that she recognized what was happening, sharing her own experience of not feeling good enough when Annie hadn't asked for help was wrong even if it was meant to offer solace, companionship, hope of a sort—it was—

Annie slowly raised her head from the paper. She was biting her lip, her great blue eyes misty, hopeful.

"Was he—did he ever get proud of you?"

Damn. Damn, damn and double damn. What could she say? Rachel didn't know, but she knew that Annie wouldn't stand for a lie.

She shook her head. "I don't know if he was proud of me," she said slowly. "But after a while, it didn't matter as much. Baseball wasn't *my* first love, and I moved on to things that pleased *me,* things that I was good at and that made *me* happy."

Annie's eyes dimmed. She frowned and sank lower in her chair. She pulled her needle-sharp little elbows into her body like a small, soft creature retreating into its shell. The answer had clearly not been the one she was seeking.

Perhaps she shouldn't have spoken, Rachel thought. But to watch that child sitting there day after day, trying to win her mother's love, working to be good enough when it was plain as white paint that she was a treasure of a child already—Rachel just couldn't do it.

"You draw beautifully, Annie," she said softly, and her words were no lie. It was obvious that the child had practiced and practiced. She might not be able to compete with a talented and fully grown woman, but she was miles ahead of children several years older than herself. "Your work is absolutely lovely. I mean that. I do. And just as soon as you're done, we're going to hang that picture. We're going to frame it and put it dead center over the living room sofa."

The kitchen clock echoed in the stillness. It ticked off the seconds. Many seconds.

Annie stirred. She raised her head, her eyes narrowed in concentration.

"What—did you do? What—things did you do when you stopped playing baseball?" She said the words slowly, almost unwillingly.

"Oh." Rachel smiled reassuringly. "I'm a gardener. I love to plant things and watch them grow. How about you? What does Annie Grayson do besides draw pictures?"

Rachel could almost see the child shrink before her. The little girl shook her head. "Daddy says I'm good at lots of things, but—he's my daddy. You know?"

She *did* know. Sam would probably be proud of his daughter no matter what she did, and that was good. Wonderful. But right now Annie needed a big dose of self-confidence. And it had to come from within.

"I understand just how much your daddy loves you," Rachel agreed. "But there must be things you *like* to do. What would you be doing if you weren't drawing right now?"

Annie looked down at the picture on the table helplessly. Rachel prayed that the child would be able to come up with something.

"Do you like to build things? Or maybe you like to make things out of clay? Or maybe you're a collector?" Rachel suggested. If it took all day she would come up with something that Annie could call her own talent, her own skill.

Sadly Annie shook her head. "I have dolls and stuffed animals, but I—mostly I like to read and tell stories to Janey and Zach," she said hesitantly. "And they're just babies."

But Rachel felt an incredibly tiny glow bud within her heart. She smiled. "So you're a storyteller, a writer, Annie Grayson. That's a wonderful way to spend your time."

Annie was shaking her head sadly. "I don't write them down."

"You don't have to," Rachel agreed. "There are many storytellers in the world who only *say* their stories out loud. We'll go to the library and look some up. I'll show you."

Hanging on tightly to the now bending crayon, Annie looked up hopefully. "I'm a storyteller?"

"I'd bet my life on it, sweetheart, if that's what you like to do."

Annie clutched her crayon more fiercely. She sucked in her bottom lip so tightly that the fragile skin on her chin turned white.

"I—I think I should just keep drawing," she said, lowering her head so that her hair suddenly swung down, concealing her face from Rachel. Slowly the child forced the crayon across her paper. Her hunched shoulders invited no more intervention.

With a sigh Rachel stood. She couldn't bring herself to push any more. She respected the child's rights too much for that. But it was hard to walk away from Annie, knowing she was beating up on herself for her mother's desertion. So very hard.

Still, she did just that. She got up, forced herself to get busy doing things around the house. She took the begonia sitting on the window ledge and cleared it of dead foliage. Humming softly the way she always did, once she retreated into her favorite tasks, she found the pretty blue ceramic pot she'd brought from home, grabbed some newspapers and began to transplant the flower from the overcrowded, ugly green plastic number it had come in to the bigger, brighter one. Once the plant was seated in its new home, she filled a dipper of water and splashed some over the soil.

"There you go," she said, setting it back on the ledge as she began to clean up the mess.

"Rachel?" Annie's tiny voice came from behind Rachel, and she spun around to see the child still clutching the same crayon she had picked up earlier. The briefest of glances revealed that the little girl had not drawn a thing. She was gazing intently at the plant on the window ledge.

"It's pretty," she said simply. And then, "Do you really think I could be a storyteller?"

Something warm and melting released deep within Rachel, a bit of soft, spring snow sliding, dropping from a high, cold mountaintop onto the sun-soaked earth below.

"I think you can, Annie. I'm absolutely sure of it," she said softly, unable and unwilling to keep from smiling. "You already *are* a storyteller. Just ask Janey and Zach."

"I *could* write my stories down, couldn't I?"

"Absolutely. If you wanted to," Rachel agreed.

A small light began to creep into Annie's eyes. Her lips curved ever so slightly. "Could you—do you think maybe you could help me with spelling? I still don't spell too good."

Her heart crying tears of relief, Rachel gave a small, tight nod. "I'll get some paper."

But as she started to leave, Annie pushed her chair back. "Rachel?"

Rachel froze in mid-stride. "Yes, Annie?"

"Do you ever play baseball anymore?"

With a small sigh, Rachel nodded slowly. "Sometimes, at family picnics or on the Fourth of July. Just because I moved on to other things doesn't mean I gave up that part of my life completely, Annie. Besides, I did it for so long that I did become rather good at it. It would be a shame to waste all those years of practice."

Annie pursed her lips. She nodded. "Even if you really like to plant things the most?"

"Even then."

Placing her crayons back in the box, Annie took a deep breath. "Maybe I would like to plant things, too."

Rachel reached out and picked up a crayon that Annie had missed. She held it out to the child with a smile. "Then we'll have to do that, won't we? Definitely, Annie."

And together they searched out paper and pens. They sat down on some soft pillows Annie arranged on the floor in front of the coffee table. Because the pillows were more like the twins' bed where she was used to telling her stories, Annie explained as she scribbled and Rachel spelled out the harder words.

By the time Sam came home there was a story, complete with pictures, bound in brightly colored cardboard, hanging on the refrigerator by a ribbon.

Shyly Annie showed him her accomplishment. "Rachel says that I'm a storyteller, Daddy."

Rachel could feel the heat of Sam's gaze before she even looked up.

"That's wonderful praise, indeed, then, pumpkin. Rachel is a very wise woman."

Raising her head, Rachel stared into Sam's face. His right hand was on his daughter's hair, his left hand held the thin booklet which Annie had retrieved from its spot on the fridge. His stance, his gestures, spoke of his love for his child, but his expression was for her, for Rachel. Intense, fire bright, his eyes registered his thanks, the fact that she'd chipped a tiny hole in Annie's melancholy.

Rachel wanted to step close, to look even closer into those eyes that washed her with feeling. She wanted to lean away, remembering how his appreciation had left her reeling only a few nights ago. Sam was a passionate man, given to physical expression of his emotions.

She swayed slightly, shut her eyes against the rush of need that rose within her.

When she opened them two seconds later, Sam was seated at the table with Annie on his lap, listening to her read her story to him.

Rachel quietly left the room. She checked in on the twins, made her way back downstairs. She was just getting ready to leave when the doorbell rang.

Annie sprang up from her seat. She opened the door.

"Daddy's sent you flowers, Rachel," she announced. "Rachel likes plants." Her voice was quiet but triumphant as she turned to her father. She held the paper-wrapped creation out to Rachel.

Sam had never been there when his gifts arrived before. With shaking fingers Rachel took Annie's offering from her. She turned her back, went to the kitchen counter and opened the package to reveal a beautiful collection of mixed blossoms. Blush pink petals, rose, white, with brilliant saffron centers, their fragrance filled her senses, beckoned to her.

Closing her eyes briefly, Rachel breathed in the delicate fragrance. She touched her nose to the feathery petals and spun, prepared to do the proper thing and thank Sam.

But Sam had moved up beside her. He had seen her silly reaction to the flowers, and suddenly Rachel felt foolish. She knew hot color was tingeing her cheeks, probably turning them as rosy as the blossoms.

"You're a very thoughtful employer, Sam," she said, her voice just a trace too weak.

Sam's lips quirked up in a half smile. "I'm a very grateful employer," he said. "I'm an extremely happy father," he admitted.

"They're lovely," she whispered, holding up the flowers so that they were positioned squarely between his lips and hers.

"They're nothing," he answered, holding up Annie's storybook, and Rachel knew if Annie hadn't been standing right there he would have said so much more. He felt that his offering paled compared to hers.

"They're beautiful," she insisted. "Thank you."

"Could I smell?" Annie asked suddenly.

Grateful for the chance to break away from Sam's mesmerizing gaze, Rachel looked down at the little girl. "Of course you may, Annie. Would you like one?"

Annie looked at the flowers eagerly, then shook her head. "They're yours," she said quietly.

But Rachel pulled a fat, dusky, pink-and-white blossom from the bunch. "Flowers are for giving, for sharing," she said as she tucked it behind the child's ear and Annie ran off to see if Janey and Zach were awake so they could see her prize.

"Giving," Sam said quietly as Rachel watched the child race away. "That's what you are, Rachel. A beautiful, giving miracle worker." And following Rachel's example, he plucked one full-blown blossom from the bunch. He raised it to her mouth, stroked it slowly across her lips, across her cheek, down the line of her jaw. He stroked the sensitive skin of her throat with the soft petals, then gently eased the blossom into her hair, placing it behind her ear.

Rachel's throat felt like it was closing, her skin was aflame where he'd trailed the blossom across it. Swallowing hard, trying to press her desire down deep within her, to shatter it, she dragged her teeth across her lips.

Sam's eyes darkened to midnight blue. He stepped closer.

She reached for the knob behind her. She held out the package of flowers. "I think you can stop sending these now, Sam. I'm going to run out of vases soon," she said, trying to make her voice light and teasing.

At her tone he stepped back and away. "I'll buy you more vases, Rachel," he whispered. "If you recall, you suggested that I confine my thanks to flowers. And I *do* need to thank you."

His low, seductive voice made Rachel feel as if every nerve ending she possessed was sizzling. "I'm—I'm glad I could help," she managed, edging around the door.

She just wished to heaven that she could help herself—from feeling too much. If Sam would just cooperate, if he'd stop sending her flowers, if he'd just stop—being Sam, everything would be all right.

Sam studied the deep lavender of the orchids inhabiting the lacy china pot Cynthia was showing him and slowly nodded his approval. They were a touch more exotic than the blossoms he'd sent to Rachel thus far, but the shivering beauty of the delicate petals reminded him of her, even as he conceded that this might be a mistake. Cynthia was already jumping to conclusions about him and Rachel—the wrong conclusions. He wasn't courting the lady.

"She's taking care of my children like they were her own, Cynthia. Money just doesn't seem like enough," he said, trying to justify what he was doing when he couldn't really even explain it to himself.

"I'm not saying anything, Sam," Cynthia said, raising both brows, "but I'm sure a lot of other people have noticed all the time you've been spending here and all the flowers that have been flowing out to Rachel. None of my business, of course."

It wasn't. Or anyone else's either, and he was *not* courting the woman. Even if he *was* interested in getting involved again, which he wasn't, he'd be a fool to try with Rachel, according to Uncle Hal. Apparently every man in ten counties had tried to win her in the years since he'd been gone. Rachel was simply unwinnable. She apparently hadn't met the right man. And considering his own past history with the woman, well . . . he wasn't even thinking about getting in the long line of men waiting for Rachel.

The only reason he kept sending her these flowers when it made him look like a stupid dolt in the eyes of the world was because she seemed to enjoy them so much. That was all. He'd caught her leaning forward to breathe in their scent, he'd seen her smile when those flowers had arrived yesterday. A few baskets of blossoms and he could call forth the sweet, spontaneous enthusiasm of a Rachel he'd thought he'd known years ago—before she'd decided he made her uncomfortable.

"Catch you later, Cynthia," he said, not bothering to elaborate on his thoughts. He had enough trouble dealing with his own questions regarding his motives without taking heat from anyone else.

And when he got home a half hour later, Sam had even more questions. Such as why was everything so quiet? Why was the house all locked up with no sign of Rachel's little red hatchback? And where were his children?

Other men might have panicked, but Sam knew his kids were in good hands. It was just that—he was used to coming home to smiles and hugs, and he was getting far too used to the sound of a woman's musical voice greeting him every night.

Grumbling at the wayward thought, Sam fumbled for the key he hadn't had to use lately. Pushing into the kitchen, which seemed suddenly too big and empty, he had barely located the note which read "Bak in tin minits" in Annie's childish scribble when the roar of a car pulling into the drive drew his attention. Stepping out onto the porch, Sam watched as Annie jumped out of the passenger seat, running to the hatch of the car, hopping up and down on one foot with a level of excitement he hadn't seen in months.

"Hi, Daddy," she called, waving. "We got seeds. And flowers. And—and—what's that stuff, Rachel?"

"Peat moss, angel," Rachel answered, levering the front seat forward and leaning back to unclasp the catch that held Janey in place in her child seat. From where he stood, Sam got a first-class view of Rachel's bottom snugged tight against her jeans. He felt like the top of his head was going to blow off. Quickly he plunked his Stetson back on and tilted the brim forward to block most of the enticing sight.

"Yes, Daddy, we got peat moss," Annie announced, holding one finger up in the air to make her point. "Peat moss is very 'portant, you know, for growing things. It holds—it holds something in the dirt, doesn't it, Rachel?"

Rachel tumbled Janey and her sadly battered bear, "Baby," into her arms and placed the little girl on solid ground. Peeking over her shoulder to grin at Sam who was now lounging as casually as he could against a porch support, Rachel nodded. "You've got it exactly right, sweet stuff. We need peat moss to hold the moisture in the soil. Up and at 'em, sport," she said softly to Zach, who had fallen asleep with his head flopped over against the plastic edge of the child seat. Squatting down, she stroked the backs of her fingers lightly across his cheek until he stirred and sat forward, blinking hard. When she released him and held out her arms, he smiled sleepily and fell forward into her grasp.

Gazing down at the contented foursome on his lawn, Sam was amazed to find a lump forming in his throat. A casual onlooker would never suspect that Rachel hadn't reared his babies since birth.

"Gotcha." She laughed down at Zach, snuggling him close and smoothing his wayward hair down before carrying him to Sam.

"Dee," Zach said, as though absolutely charmed to find his father there.

Sam's heart tipped over the way it did every time he looked into his children's faces. He reached down to remove his son from Rachel's uplifted arms. "I missed you, too, tiger," he told his child.

With both his hands and Rachel's still on the boy, Sam stared into her long-lashed, gray eyes. "So you're planning a garden?" he said, using talk to cover up any awkwardness she might feel as his fingers brushed her own.

He'd been fighting himself all week, but he'd kept his hands off her. She'd been shooing men away like flies for years, and Sam didn't want to be just another pest of a man in her life. But damn, every time he got within six feet of Rachel, a sharp spear of need rose within him. And Sam knew that he was headed for quicksand, because while he might not want to get emotionally involved with a woman again, while he'd learned that he didn't know the first thing about what women wanted, *he* wanted Rachel in the worst way. And there was no way he was ever going to have her.

"Oh, not just any old garden, Sam," she said, her eyes glowing as she smiled up at him impishly. "Tell him, Annie," she said as the little girl moved closer, holding her sister by the hand.

"We are going to have a monster garden, Daddy. The biggest. The best. With lots and lots and lots of flowers. Pansies and daisies and mary-golds and—" She frowned, then tried again. "And belly buttons," she finished triumphantly.

Sam swallowed his laugh as he watched a smiling Rachel lean in close to whisper in Annie's ear. For two whole seconds the bright hair of the woman and child flowed together, and then Annie turned to Rachel questioningly and Rachel smiled back, nodding encouragement.

"Bachelor buttons," she said, correcting herself.

"Yes," Rachel agreed. "And roses. You're going to have such roses. There are already some on the side of the house but they're practically choking, poor babies. We'll fix them up, though. You'll love it, Sam. Roses are perfect for this lovely old house."

"Woses," Janey said solemnly. "Woses, woses, woses."

"Exactly, Janey love," Rachel said, brushing her finger across the little girl's nose. "Lots of roses for Janey."

"Well." Sam beamed, sitting down on the top step of the porch so that Zach could take his freedom or leave it. "It looks like you're all going to be plenty busy tomorrow. And roses, eh? I remember how Aunt Esther always had roses around her porch. Red and pink and yellow. You could tell you were getting close to Uncle Hal's just by breathing in deeply on a summer's night."

When he stopped speaking, he found himself looking directly into Rachel's face. Her lips were slightly parted, there was a wistful look about her eyes.

"This is going to be a real home, just like Hal and Esther's was, Sam. I remember that place, too. It *was* wonderful, but I think that had more to do with your aunt and uncle than the flowers. Still, all those blossoms didn't hurt."

"Did you have roses at your house when you were a girl, Rachel?" Annie's voice piped up, and Sam shifted over so she could sit beside him on the porch. He pulled Janey down on his other knee.

"Absolutely always," Rachel agreed, laughing. "Even when we didn't have food, my mother always made sure we had flowers. She tended her roses, and she saved the seeds from the other plants every year."

"You didn't have food?" Annie's voice rose, clearly shocked at such a statement.

"Annie!" he admonished, but Rachel shook her head to stop him.

Sam was still gazing directly at Rachel, but at his daughter's words, he noticed that she had shifted her focus slightly to the right so she was no longer looking directly in his eyes. She had stuffed her hands into her front pockets as though to keep them still. She looked absolutely uncomfortable, but after just a few seconds a small chuckle escaped her, and she looked down at him and shrugged impishly.

"Don't censure her, Sam, when it was my own fault for walking right into that one. Besides, while it was true, you know, I can't remember it mattering all that much. There was always *something* to eat, even if it wasn't anything particularly tasty, and my mother—she just always made everything bright for all of us somehow. We knew she loved us so much and she was always encouraging us. It just didn't always seem like we were poor. I'm not sure I can explain it."

She was explaining it beautifully. Sam understood perfectly about a woman who could make things bright for everyone. He was looking at her right now.

"Daddy." Annie was tugging on the leg of his jeans. "Can't we plant something tonight? Just one flower?"

Sam looked down into his daughter's eager eyes. "All right, after Rachel goes we'll—"

"No. No, we have to have Rachel. She's the one who knows how to plant the stuff. Uncle Hal says she has a magic green thumb."

Sam looked across at Rachel, who had the grace to look embarrassed. She held up her thumb. "Uncle Hal exaggerates now and then, Annie, just to be nice, but I *will* stay awhile, Sam, if you don't mind. You can't go out and buy flowers and then not plant even one."

She sounded almost as eager as Annie.

He looked down at the twins, hoping they were falling asleep. Nope. They looked like they were ready to eat dirt, too.

"All right. I'm outvoted," he said, rising and placing the little ones on the porch. "Lead me to the shovels. I'm yours to command. Even though," he said, cupping his hand around his mouth as though he was conveying a secret, "I have to tell you that I spent my growing years working with wood, the kind that was already out of the ground."

"No magic green thumb?" Rachel asked sympathetically.

"Worse. *All* thumbs where gardening's concerned," he admitted, grinning broadly.

But when Rachel reached out to examine the hands he was holding out, when she touched just the tip of one finger to the pad of his thumb, Sam's grin died an instant death. He

didn't know if the woman really had a green thumb, but he knew for sure that there was magic in her touch—and it was killing him, inch by painful inch as he fought back the urge to slide his hands forward, grasp her wrists and turn that tentative touch into solid sensation.

It was going to be a long evening, even longer than he had anticipated when he'd agreed to this project, Sam thought. Thank goodness Annie had insisted on planting only few flowers.

The sun was almost a memory by the time Rachel and Annie patted the dirt down around the last marigold. Sam stood to one side, leaning on the shovel he'd been wielding all evening.

Rachel tilted her head back, looking up at him from the place where she was kneeling on the ground.

"Just a few flowers, Rachel?" he asked.

She held both hands out, palms up, with a helpless shrug. "I guess we did get a little carried away," she admitted. "But there's just something wondrous about planting a flower. Knowing that that little seed, that small plant, will come out of hiding, rise up and stretch to the sun, reaching for what it needs and wants, always amazes me no matter how many times I see it happen."

Rachel shrugged, a bit embarrassed at her own enthusiasm. "Still, I can see that maybe we shouldn't have planted quite so many this late at night," she agreed, looking over the flower-dappled beds.

But the truth was that Annie had been so excited that Rachel just couldn't have spoiled the little girl's fun by calling a halt to things. She'd shaken off Sam's attempts to get her home at a decent hour several times as she and Annie discussed the merits of planting things in rows versus a more random pattern.

Annie had fluttered around like a dirty little butterfly, rotating between making sure that Janey and Zach were okay and losing herself in the fun of fostering life in the earth.

Since Janey and Zach were perfectly content to wallow in dirt and bunch the wet soil between their chubby fists, Annie soon forgot everything but the plants and seeds.

And that was the way it should be, Rachel thought. Annie was, for once, acting like a child.

Now as the little girl gathered up the spades and carried them to the shed behind the house, Rachel started to attempt to rise after being on her knees for several hours.

"Here. Let me help."

Looking up, she saw Sam's hand outstretched to grasp her own. For long seconds she just looked. After foolishly touching him earlier this evening and feeling the kick of desire deep within her, she was reluctant to have physical contact with him in any way. But they'd worked together side by side for hours, it was late, the kids were hungry and tired and—she was holding up the show by being silly.

Carefully she placed her hand in Sam's much bigger one. The warmth closed around her as Sam tugged and she came up, pitching forward against his chest.

For three whole seconds she lay there, her breasts pressing into the hard muscles she remembered all too well. She breathed in the scent of Sam, she felt her head begin to swirl—and then she was standing on her own feet as he carefully placed her away from him.

"Thank—thank you," she whispered.

"I'd do it for anyone," he said, and for some reason she thought Sam sounded a bit angry. But she must have been mistaken, for in the next breath, he was lifting the twins high into his arms.

"We'd better get you home, Rachel. It's late. I shouldn't have let this go on so long. You're probably dead on your feet."

Dead wasn't the word for what Rachel was feeling. It was the way she'd felt only seconds ago—before her encounter with Sam's warm body. Now she felt awake, alive—confused.

This was not supposed to be happening again. For days now she'd been concentrating on remembering Don. She'd already decided he *had* been right. When they'd met for the first time, it had been too soon after her mother's death. Her emotions had been numb. She wouldn't have responded to *any* man. Even Sam couldn't have stirred her then, and things would be different when Don came back. She'd thought about calling him once or twice; she'd known that he would come if she did. But she had to be sure, she would never want to hurt someone as sweet as Don had been. Still, in spite of her hesitation, she was sure he must have been right. Her emotions had just been numb last time.

They weren't feeling numb at all right now, Rachel thought, looking at Sam's broad back as he walked away from her with a twin in each arm. He was a strong man, yet he held those babies like precious china. He rubbed his cheek up against their baby skin lightly, so as not to hurt them. He listened to their cooing noises and talked back to them as if he understood every word.

Rachel closed her eyes quickly. She tried to concentrate on Don.

"This was fun, Rachel."

Annie's tired little voice sounded behind her, and Rachel turned to see the child looking wanly up at her, her legs almost wobbling.

Quickly Rachel reached out. She forgot her cardinal rule of not touching a shy child until she had been asked. Drawing Annie near, Rachel braced an arm around the little girl's shoulders, encouraging her to walk, holding her up and taking most of the child's weight upon herself.

"You know, Annie, I think you just might have a magic green thumb yourself," she whispered as they neared the house. "Come on, I'll whip up something real quick for you to eat, and then we'll get you cleaned up and in bed. It's been quite a day."

"I liked it," the child confided. "Did you?"

Rachel tried not to notice that Annie's voice wobbled a little on her question. Her own answer was inevitable.

"I loved it, Annie. Every minute."

A shy smile crept onto the little girl's face as she breathed out what could only be relief. The next time Rachel looked down the little girl's head was bobbing down to her chin. Rachel slid her arm tighter around the child's body and lifted her off her feet. Annie was asleep before they made it inside.

Swinging the child up into her arms, Rachel put her foot on the first tread just as Sam stepped back out the door.

"Let me," he whispered. "A six-year-old is quite a handful."

Rachel would have argued, but Sam already had Annie half in his grasp. She nodded, dragging her own feet up the steps.

Inside the living room, the twins still babbled away, but with a little less vigor than before.

Sam was looking down into his daughter's face. Annie was smiling in her sleep.

"You're a heck of a woman, Rachel," he said. "But then I suppose plenty of people have told you that."

"Why? Because I managed to send your daughter to sleep without dinner? And the twins' feet! Just look at those crusty little toes."

Sam chuckled low as he stared at where Rachel was pointing. "Don't worry, Rachel. It's mud. I'll throw them in the tub in a moment. And you can't say that any of them went to bed unhappy tonight. Annie had a blast. She's never done anything of this magnitude before."

"Yes, well, digging in the ground is very elemental, I guess," she said. "The ground is solid. Immovable. It's security of a sort. And you can just forget about plopping those babies in the tub and sending me home until I've given them at least a little something to eat. I can't send them to bed hungry."

Sam shook his head. "I'll take care of everything." He frowned menacingly.

Rachel frowned right back.

She stood there holding her ground for long seconds, trying to look stern in the face of Sam's objections to her staying.

"I'm not charging you overtime for the extra time, Sam."

"As if I wouldn't pay you, when you've beat your tail off."

The thought dug in. She'd been hiring out as a sitter for years. Somehow she didn't want money for this night, for Annie's triumph.

"No money for tonight," she said stubbornly.

"They're *my* children," he insisted.

"They're my—I—it would hurt to take money for tonight," she ended lamely. "It was fun for me, too, anyway."

She saw that Sam was studying the situation, trying to decide what was the right thing to do.

"And while you're giving in," she said, grasping the opportunity, "why don't you go start the bathwater. I'm already making something for them to eat." And without letting him have the chance to object, she slipped out the door and into the kitchen, safely away from the lure of Sam and his babies. With the night closing around them, binding them, she felt somehow shut off in a world where there was only Sam and his children. It was an alluring world, warm and enticing—and off-limits. It was important to remember that this was only one night, not a lifetime. And in less than an hour she'd be back in her own apartment—far away from all this temptation.

Chapter Six

Standing in the twins' bedroom, Rachel smiled in the darkness. A low, muffled chuckle came from Sam. Zach had just flipped over, hoisting his bottom in the air. Janey was snoring with Baby crushed in her arms.

It had taken both her and Sam to get everyone fed, bathed and in bed. For the sake of speed and the children's much-needed rest, not to mention the fact that she had latched on to the idea like a pit bull, Sam had agreed to let her help him with the nighttime routine.

Now it was pitch-black as they both tiptoed outside, shutting the twins' door behind them.

"They're wonderful children, Sam," she said quietly. "Absolutely adorable."

"You mean I don't just feel that way because I'm their father?" he asked, smiling in the low lamplight he'd clicked on.

"Guess not, because they've got me eating out of their hands," she confessed.

"Not when they're muddy, I hope," Sam said, raising his brows.

"Even then," she confessed. "Do they ever hear from their mother—at all? I mean, it's none of my business, but—"

"Shh," he said, touching her lips with one finger. "Of course it's your business when you're with them all the time. But no, she never writes, she never calls. I don't really understand how—" He flattened one hand against the door frame and blew out a breath, voicing his frustration without words.

"Maybe—" Rachel stopped, then tried again. "Maybe she'd like to, but she just can't begin to explain to them how she could have gone in the first place. Maybe she doesn't understand it, either...."

"You're excusing her?"

Rachel shook her head. "No, not at all. Walking out the door without a word, leaving her children alone without any answers to their questions—there can't be any excuse for that. I guess it's just natural to want to make some sense out of the situation. I never really knew much about Donna. She was two years older than me, and we didn't travel in the same crowd. All I remember is that she was pretty, the prom queen. Maybe she was just too young to be married. Maybe she didn't really know what she wanted."

Sam hooked his thumbs in his front pockets, he blew out a deep breath, then looked up, out into the darkness beyond the window. "I don't know—hell, I don't know anything, and obviously knew even less back then."

When he turned to her, Rachel froze. The memory of a day ten years ago when she'd walked off the dance floor with no explanation, leaving Sam alone in the midst of a crowd, slipped into her mind. And, looking up into Sam's suddenly dark eyes, she wondered if he was thinking the same thing. Of course, he wouldn't be.

He took a step forward.

Rachel opened her mouth as though to speak, then closed it again as Sam stepped closer still.

She looked for words but they disappeared in Sam's dark blue eyes. And after all, it was only her own guilty imagination suggesting that he even wanted an explanation, that he even cared why she had deserted him that day.

It had been a simple, small incident ten years ago, nearly forgotten. Best forgotten.

The only thing to remember was right here, right now, who she was, who *he* was, when there was no possibility for more. A safe relationship, uncomplicated, with no need for explanations . . . or emotions.

As Sam stepped forward, holding out his hand as though he meant to slip it along her waist and take that long-ago dance, Rachel held her breath. But at the touch of his fingers claiming her, wooing her, making her mind whirl like a speeding carnival ride, she took a small step back. She pulled into herself, turned and made her escape, hunting in her pocket for her keys.

"It's awfully late, Sam," she said, her voice strained and throaty, her lips stiff, barely functioning. "Tomorrow will be here before we know it."

A long silence followed her words. She risked a glance back over her shoulder to where Sam was still watching her.

"Yes," he said, frowning and shoving a hand back through his hair. "It's much too late, I guess."

Rachel lay in her bed, trying to shove Sam Grayson back into the corners of her mind where he rightfully belonged.

She counted sheep, she did advanced algebra problems in her head, but the man just refused to be shoved. No matter how hard she tried, she could still see him pushing that Stetson back on his head and staring her up and down just as clearly as if he was standing before her. She could still feel the heat of his hand at her waist.

"Come on, stop acting like a total doofus, Rachel," she told herself, punching her pillow for the fiftieth time as she rolled over once again, staring into the darkness. Heavens, the man was her employer. He'd made no attempt to even get close to her again since she'd run out into the night over a week ago. If she was smart, she'd definitely put him out of her mind.

But when she closed her eyes, she saw instead Sam trying to put Zach's socks on, Sam carrying Annie into the house. She felt Sam's lips on her own and groaned. Sitting up, she gave up on sleep entirely. There was just something about that man that nagged at her, and she wished to heck he'd just stop.

Unfortunately, Rachel thought, dragging out a book on floristry as a business, she wasn't sure what it was that she wanted Sam to stop. He hadn't touched her since that night a week ago, hadn't even tried. He'd allowed their relationship to become strictly business. There wasn't a thing she could think of that he could do to change things—except disappear into thin air. Even then, she'd probably sit up nights wondering what had happened to him. She was just going to have to give time a chance to work its magic. In a month or two or three, she probably wouldn't even notice Sam anymore.

Rolling her eyes at that ludicrous thought, Rachel focused on the chapter entitled "Accounting Procedures." Within five minutes she was yawning and putting her book aside. She wondered what Sam would think if he knew that he kept her awake at night. Moot point, she decided, because Sam was never, ever going to know how he affected her. He wouldn't get the chance, because she was going to continue to keep her distance from that pesky man who kept popping up in her dreams.

"It's time, Rachel," she assured herself as she sank deeper into the pillows. With the passing of the last few days, Annie had begun to grow used to her new home and her new situation. She was beginning to chat, to smile more and more. It was time to introduce her to the community and other children . . . to begin the whole process of bringing Annie full circle, back into life. And when that was done, Rachel would have to step aside, out of that little girl's life, or risk becoming too big a part of it, a hindrance rather than a help. Then she would find someone to care for Janey and Zach on a permanent basis. She would walk away from Sam's world . . . and away from Sam.

Again.

That pesky man. She missed him already. But he would never know.

The sound of the phone on the nightstand woke Rachel at seven the next morning.

Groggy, she rolled over and grabbed for it, knocking the receiver off and sending it skidding over the wood.

"Hello," she finally managed to say, shoving the mouthpiece up under her long, tangled hair.

"Hey, Rachel," a creaky voice rasped. "Sorry to wake you up on a Saturday morning, but I heard that you were looking for some lilacs to set off that big, white house of Sam's. Truck just came in with the most beautiful spread of bushes you ever did see. Thought you might like some before the crowds come in and they're all picked over. These babies are somethin', all right."

"Ray?" Rachel said on a yawn. Ray owned the local hardware store, and he was a lifelong friend. Secretly she'd always thought he'd been just a little in love with her mother. "Thanks, Ray," she said, after the man had elaborated a bit more on just how great these lilacs were. "I'll have to see if Sam wants to have a look at them. If not, save one for me, anyway. A person can't have too many lilacs."

Ray laughed. "I can see Sam's in trouble already. I'll just set a few of the better ones off on the side."

Hanging up the phone, Rachel swung her bare legs over the bed and sat staring at the phone. She didn't really want to call Sam. She shouldn't call him. Not at all.

No, remembering the way it had been the last time she'd gone too near the man, she didn't even want to think "Sam." What's more, it was Saturday, and she wasn't scheduled to work on the weekends, but...Ray had been right about the effect of whitewood and lilacs. Besides, Annie and the twins would love the scent of the blossoms and—and it *was* Saturday. Everyone would be in town. All the kids would be at the playground. It was a good time to ease Annie into new relationships in a nonthreatening way.

Her enthusiasm had nothing to do with Sam himself or the I-want-you look she'd imagined she'd seen in his eyes last week. No, she was calling him simply because she was being a good neighbor, a faithful employee and his sister's friend. Those were the only reasons.

And that was why, less than an hour later, Rachel found herself packed into the passenger side of the Grayson family van. She looked tentatively across the width of the van to where Sam was staring at her as he revved up the engine.

"Lilacs?" he asked, raising one brow and tipping his hat down over eyes that still blazed blue even this early in the morning. "You think we need lilacs at eight in the morning?"

"I love lilacs," Annie said dreamily from her spot in the back between the twins.

Rachel stared at him, smiling. "Well?" she asked.

"You know, I always did like lilacs," he agreed. "Almost as much as I like roses. It's just that—well, I kind of like to wake up slow and smooth on the weekends, Rachel. Preferably with a cup of hot coffee," he admitted on a groan. "This couldn't have waited ten minutes, could it?"

He sounded so frustrated that Rachel almost reached out to console him with a touch. But she remembered too well the feel of muscle and bone and soft masculine hair beneath her palm. She knew that if she touched him, Sam would turn those soul-searching eyes on her. So she didn't touch.

"Poor Sam," she said instead. "I'm sorry I rolled you out of bed without even so much as one breath of caffeine. But don't worry. Ray always opens up early on the weekends, and he'll have plenty of coffee brewing. I promise you. Strong stuff guaranteed to grow hair in all the places you'd rather not have any."

Sam's laughter was deep and husky. "That's what I like," he said, quirking one brow. "A woman who promises me buckets of coffee and a hairy body."

"And lilacs," she reminded him.

"Lilacs, too," he agreed, ignoring her superior look. "By the way, I *was* going in to see Ray today, anyway," he told her. "Later, though. Much later."

Rachel looked askance at him.

He shrugged sheepishly. "I thought maybe I'd rototill a plot of ground over on the back corner of the lot. I remember you saying that the kids might like a vegetable garden. Thought we'd try it."

"We?" Her voice nearly squeaked over the word.

"The kids and me," he clarified, his voice perfectly expressionless. "Of course, it wouldn't hurt to have the expert advice of someone who has a magic green thumb."

Rachel couldn't stop her smile. "We'll pick up some seeds today," she agreed, soothingly. "It's a good idea, Sam. You're a good father."

"I wasn't fishing for compliments," he assured her.

"I know. I was just stating the obvious."

He glanced her way and tilted his head in a silent thank you. Just then Zach decided it was time to sing a song. Within a few minutes, everyone was joining in on a chorus of Old MacDonald. Of course, the only words the twins knew were the "Ee-i-ee-i-oh's," but they joined in with great relish and a tremendous amount of noise when their parts came up.

Pulling into town with the windows rolled down and the enthusiastic but less-than-melodic music pouring out onto the streets of Tucker, Rachel shook her head and smiled. She was glad that she had listened to her heart and not her mind this morning and called Sam. A Grayson sing-along was not to be missed, and at the moment, she felt just like a Grayson. A temporary, but very real part of this family. It was important that she remember the "temporary" part.

Sam swung down out of the van and circled around the back to help Rachel get the kids out of their seats. He thanked his shining stars for Ray and his lilac bushes. For the last week and more, he'd been kicking himself for that last stupid act of his and trying to find out some way to patch things up with Rachel without looking like even more of a jerk. She'd been all business this past week, leaving just as soon as he got home, but today, when she'd called—heck, there was just something that felt right about this day, something that fit like jeans that had been worn to white comfort.

Last night he had gone to bed still wondering just how badly he'd dented his relationship with Rachel by stepping over the line again. Now it was as if he'd never even touched her. He wondered if that was what she was trying to do, make him forget that they *had* ever touched. Sam frowned at the ridiculous thought.

But then, trying to figure out Rachel Allyn's motives had always been incredibly frustrating. He shouldn't even be trying now. For sure he shouldn't be reading too much into the fact that it was Rachel who had sought him out today. If he was smart, he'd just pick up his lilacs, his seeds and his Rototiller and then hustle the woman back to her house as fast as possible. He'd give her an extra paycheck for working a Saturday, and everyone would be happy.

"Lead me to those lilacs," he said, handing Zach into her arms as he took Janey and grasped Annie by the hand.

"Don't you want a cup of coffee first, Sam?" she asked, flooding her voice with mock sympathy.

Sam took a good look at Rachel. Her long jeans-clad legs were parted as she rocked Zach back and forth, the white short sleeve of her sweater was pushed up where Zach had dragged against her, the soft honeyed skin of her upper arm was exposed. It was just a bare arm, Sam told himself. She was just a woman holding his child, but when she tilted her head, awaiting his response, and her hair slid across her throat, creating a peekaboo web of dark silk and pale, naked skin, Sam found that coffee was the last thing on his mind.

"You bet I want coffee, lady," he said. "Lead me to it."

Pouring out a cup of Ray's finest overbrewed, thick-as-mud, stick-in-your-throat java, Sam nodded as Rachel signaled that she was going to take the kids and go search out her treasure.

He watched as she placed Janey and Zach in a cart and made her way between the long tables of bedding plants. Along the way she and Annie stopped and discussed the flowers. He could see his daughter's animated hand signals as she moved off into the distance.

And he saw the way men stopped what they were doing to take a closer look at Rachel, as if she hadn't been in here a thousand times, as if they'd never had the chance to notice that she could make a man's tongue melt in his mouth.

The half-empty cup crushed in on itself as he squeezed too tightly, and hot coffee sloshed over the edges.

Sam tossed the whole mess in a nearby garbage can and started purposefully in the direction his family had gone.

"Look, Daddy. Trees," Annie said, pointing to an area at the edge of the bedding plants. "Can I take Janey and Zach to see?"

Sam laughed and nodded as Rachel turned the cart over to Annie.

After the children had gone, a strong silence began to spread out and surround the two of them. Sam let it spread. This was the first time, not counting the ride over, that he'd gotten within ten feet of the woman in the last week.

He realized, with some amazement, that he'd missed having her near. She was a pleasure just to look at, but more than that, there was a sort of sunshine that surrounded her. He found himself wanting some of that buttery warmth for himself.

"You fit into this town as if you'd been planted here," he said quietly, thumbing the petal of a nearby geranium.

A bubbly laugh escaped her. "I'm not quite sure if that's a compliment or an insult," Rachel said.

"Definitely a compliment," he agreed. "It just means that I recognize your worth, Rachel. And I thank you for coming out on a day when you didn't have to."

She shrugged. "Well—I guess I just go with the flow. As Ray says, those lilacs won't last forever, so we'd better get a move on. Besides, I thought we might take the kids over to the playground afterward. There'll be plenty of children over there today," she suggested.

He let his gaze rest on her, drinking in the softness in her eyes for as long as he could, before he was forced to speak.

"That sounds like just the ticket, Rachel," he agreed, his voice a bit more gravelly than he had intended. "But are you sure about the playground? After all, this is supposed to be your day off."

The small hesitation before she nodded was almost imperceptible. Another man might not have noted it, but then another man might not have been looking at Rachel as closely as Sam always did.

He blew out a breath, realizing just how much time he spent actually studying Rachel's expressions. He guessed it had always been like that. Even when she'd been just a kid, too young for him to have thought of her as anything else, he'd spent a lot of time reading her reactions to him.

"What if I take you home and then bring the kids back?" he suggested. It wasn't what he wanted, but it was clearly the right thing to do.

To his surprise she shook her head.

"I promised Annie I'd introduce her around. Do you think I'd just dump her on a playground full of kids I already know without giving her a proper introduction?"

The woman never quit, did she? First she showed up on a Saturday morning so that she could help her plant-ignorant employer pick out lilac bushes, then she insisted on playing social secretary for his daughter.

Not that Sam was complaining. He'd missed sparring with her. He'd missed standing close enough to see the glitter in those gray eyes of hers. And even though he'd only experienced it once before, already he missed the feel of her lips moving beneath his own.

"No, I don't think you'd do anything that you think would hurt Annie," he said, tilting one corner of his lips up. "But I do think you might beat me to death with a lilac bush if I ever even suggested such a thing. I was just trying to show you some consideration, Rachel. You're not my slave. You're my..."

What was she really, anyway? It was obvious that she was his employee, but he'd had other employees, and Sam couldn't think of a single one who'd ever affected him the way this one slender woman had.

Moreover, as his words trailed off and Rachel waited expectantly, he could almost swear he saw a look in her eyes that caught him totally off guard. She looked like a woman with more on her mind than lilacs and babies, she looked the way he was feeling inside, as if somewhere a small match was glowing within her.

The thought that she might want him back left Sam stunned—and burning.

Within less than a breath, she had blinked, extinguished that glow he'd thought he recognized.

"We'd better go get the children and the plants," she said quickly, her color high. "Ray will set the bushes aside for us until we get back from the playground and then I—I really should get home," she concluded lamely.

Home. Her home. Not his home. And Sam knew suddenly, without a doubt he wanted her in his own home. He *wanted* her, plain and simple. But of course, that was out of the question. She worked for him, that was all. That was all this would ever be. You couldn't ask a woman to marry you just because she made your eyeballs steam over whenever she looked your way, could you? And he didn't want to get married again, anyway, did he? He didn't want to wake up with a note on his pillow a second time—and Rachel had always shown definite signs of I-want-to-leave tendencies whenever he was around.

"Let's go," he agreed curtly. "With a little luck we'll have you back on your front porch in just over an hour."

Rachel stood side by side with Sam, each pushing a twin in one of the baby swings at the playground.

Zach and Janey giggled and kicked their feet. They held their chins up as the wind rushed at them. It was clear they were enjoying themselves.

Watching Annie, who had settled down next to Cynthia Watts's little girl to dig in the sand, pleasure rushed over Rachel. Every now and then Annie would look back to make sure that she and Sam were still there, but not nearly as often as she might have a week ago, Rachel was sure. Sam had been right to bring his babies to this town. There *was* something about this place, something sturdy and reassuring.

There was also something about Sam. The thought darted in as Rachel watched him bracing his hands against the back of Zach's swing with every push. Sam had big hands, capable and strong. Yet she'd seen him touch his children with infinite care. And when he'd held her in his arms, he'd gentled that strength. When he could have crushed her, he'd caressed.

A shiver ran through Rachel. It was time to get control of her wayward thoughts. She was trying to read Sam, even knowing that she'd read him wrong once before and gotten hurt as a result. Sam might be older, but he was still the man who had thought her a sorry little puppy and had taken pity on her. And if she hadn't forgotten that, had he? Was she still that poor little Allyn kid in the back of Sam's mind?

No, she didn't think so. Time and her own determination had changed her circumstances. But that didn't mean she could drop her defenses one bit around Sam. He didn't want or need the same things she did. She was looking for a long-term relationship, wouldn't settle for less than heart-and-soul, till-death-do-us-part love. And Sam? Sam might want a housekeeper, a baby-sitter, maybe even a lover—but not more. And she couldn't think about Sam as a lover, refused to remember his supple fingers, his questing lips upon her skin. She would think about anything else but that.

"Is everything going well down at the lumberyard?" she asked, hoping she sounded calm. "Uncle Hal is absolutely ecstatic to have you back."

Sam gave Zach another push. "It's good to be with him again. When I was young, I don't think I appreciated the business or just how much he knows about it. But now I can see what a fine job he's done of keeping things humming. He knows all his customers and all of their kids' names. He knows the lumber business like nobody else. I'm lucky he wanted me back after being gone so long, and yes, everything's going great guns. It's good to be home. No regrets."

Not like her, Rachel thought. And no, she didn't regret Sam's coming home, not like she'd thought she would. She loved watching his children, she loved watching and talking to Sam. But she *did* have regrets, and they had more to do with her own inability to control her reactions to Sam and his family than anything else. It wasn't his fault she'd always had this weakness where he was concerned.

And she shouldn't beat herself up about it, either. At least with Sam she had a living model of what she was looking for in a husband. She'd know when she hit pay dirt without even thinking twice.

"Okay, switch!" Sam said suddenly, catching her off guard.

In a heartbeat, he was in her space, standing right behind her.

"You're supposed to move over to the other swing, darlin'," he said, leaning down to whisper near her ear.

"I knew that," she managed, feeling her neck begin to tingle, wishing Sam would move away. He didn't.

Carefully she stepped back, sidled over to where Zach's swing was already beginning to slow down. "You just caught me off guard, Sam Grayson."

"You were daydreaming."

"Yes," she said, as her breathing calmed and she dished up a smile. "I was dreaming of new forms of torture for men who catch unsuspecting women off guard."

"Sounds...exciting." He leaned a bit closer even as he gave Janey a push that made the little girl laugh with delight.

"You think cleaning toilet bowls is exciting?" she asked, leaning back and grinning up at him. "Is this a deep, dark secret you've been hiding from me?"

"Toilet bowls?" Sam howled, making Janey giggle even harder.

"Yep, that was what I was thinking. Every time a man steps out of line, he ought to be placed on latrine duty. It's a most humbling occupation," Rachel assured him.

"You think I've never been humbled in my life?" He stared her dead in the eye, and immediately Rachel remembered all the times she'd slid away whenever Sam had come near. She'd always been thinking of those times in terms of protecting herself. She'd carefully avoided looking at them from Sam's viewpoint—or else she'd assumed she hadn't had the power to wound him. But he was human, just as human as she was...and maybe she'd been wrong.

Now, with Sam pinioning her with his gaze, she found herself wanting to run away again as she'd done all those years ago. But she wouldn't. He had hired a woman, not a shadow who slipped away whenever it was convenient.

Managing to hang on to her smile, to keep her tone light, Rachel lifted one shoulder, conceding his point. "Sam, I'm sure any man who has children has been humbled many times." She lifted one brow as if to ask "Am I right?"

Sam groaned.

"I just hope Annie hasn't been telling you about the time I tried to sew her a dress, or the accident with the load of red and white clothes."

"Nope," she agreed, lifting a now squirming Zach out of the swing. "But thanks for telling me about those incidents. Now that you've piqued my interest, I'll be sure to pump Annie for all the humiliating details," she teased.

As if she'd heard her name from all the way across the playground, Annie came running. She hopped back and forth from Sam to Rachel and back again. Finally ending up next to Rachel's knees, the little girl moved in close, barely touching Rachel's free hand with the tips of her fingers.

It was the first time she'd ever initiated any kind of contact. It was a small, very small, but significant moment of trust.

Rachel almost closed her eyes, the pleasure of Annie's innocent acceptance was so intense, but she could feel Sam's gaze on her. Turning to him, she caught his look of approval.

Biting down on her lip, Annie looked up at Rachel. "Could we have Nicky over next week one day?" she asked, wiggling as if she was unsure of the response. "I want to show her my room with the window seat where my stuffed animals sleep. She could bring her new doll to show me. We would be very quiet and not make any extra work."

Rachel pressed the little girl's fingers gently. "I *want* you to invite friends over whenever you wish, Annie. And you most certainly will not be very quiet. The only rule I have is that no one intentionally hurts anyone else, so you invite Nicky, and when she comes, you'll get as messy and be as noisy as can be. We'll make cookies the day before if you like."

"Eat?" Janey asked, leaning over from the loop of Sam's arms to put her nose up next to Rachel's face.

Sam's chuckle penetrated Janey's body, so that Rachel could swear she felt it echoing inside her heart. "You bet it's time to eat, pumpkin," he said. "What do you say to lunch?"

Although his words were directed to Janey, Rachel looked up and saw that Sam was staring into her own eyes. She could feel Annie's fingers wiggling against the back of her hand, Zach's warm little bottom resting against her arm. And with Janey's cheek next to her own, and Sam . . . what on earth did it mean when Sam's blue eyes turned dark like that? Rachel didn't know, but for a few bright seconds, closed in the circle of Sam's family, Rachel felt like she belonged to him and his.

With a jolt she remembered that she'd experienced that same feeling years ago. She'd been so sure that she'd been right.

But she'd been wrong. Sam hadn't wanted her then. It wasn't love that he wanted from her now.

And it wouldn't do to forget that again...or to read more into Sam's looks than would ever be there.

"Eat," Zach agreed with great solemnity.

"Let's go then," Sam answered, planting his palm on the small of Rachel's back, turning her toward his van...toward his home.

With a slow ache she didn't want to explore forming within her throat, Rachel followed along. She knew now that she had to be very careful, so much more careful than she had realized. For Sam had come home—and she could no longer deny that his attraction for her had not died, but grown.

He was passionate, kind, he made magic for her when she watched him move or smile or whisper in his babies' ears.

She'd chased after magic all of her life, held to its promise, cherished it and made it a part of her.

But Sam was forbidden magic. Not hers.

Except—she'd been granted this very short time with him. She'd taken it, been forced to it. And she would not turn her face away. Not yet.

"Let's go home, sweetheart," she whispered into Zach's baby soft curls. For now she would indulge herself, just for now she would pretend she was a part of this family, so that she would have some memories of them to keep, memories to hold close until she had her own babies to rock, her own man to love in the nighttime.

One day she would find the man really meant for her, and she would give him all of her passion. But for this short time, Sam was here. He blotted out all others. Indulging herself, she let it be. It was all right—for now.

Chapter Seven

Sam nearly had his brood to the van, all except Annie who was watching Ray cart out the lilacs, when a woman touched Rachel on the sleeve and called her by name. Turning, Sam caught an eager look on the lady's face.

"Rachel, I've been meaning to call you," the woman said as soon as Rachel had greeted her. "I just wanted to let you know that I've had a letter from my cousin, Don. He's coming for a visit next week, and well, he wanted to write you himself, but..."

She held out her hands. "I don't know, something about keeping his word about a full year's breathing space. I'm not sure what that means. He said that *you* would. Anyway, I thought you should know that he's coming, and that he's doing well. Just made partner in the law firm. We'll look forward to having you over again." She smiled at Rachel, then turned to Zach as though she had just noticed him dangling from Rachel's arms.

"What a sweetie," she cooed as Rachel thanked her and said her goodbyes.

Sam noticed that the color on Rachel's high cheekbones was a delightful shade of rose. He didn't have a doubt as to who this unfamiliar woman was. Hal had gone on at length about Rachel's persistent suitor of the summer before. Up until now he hadn't thought much about it. There were plenty of other eager young bucks who were already sniffing around the lady, and she'd had the chance to marry this guy before and hadn't done so.

Still, her color was high. For a short moment Sam felt a twisting deep inside him, wondering if those rose-tinted cheeks signified embarrassment or eagerness. Maybe she was planning on saying yes this time...maybe she'd had good reason for waiting and he'd be dancing at *her* wedding sometime soon.

"Oww," Janey whimpered as Sam jerked at the thought, his grip tightening just a touch.

Instantly he loosened his hold and kissed the top of his daughter's bright curls.

"I'm sorry, angel," he soothed. "Let Daddy see." Lifting Janey's chubby little wrist, he was relieved to see that he hadn't really hurt his child, but he placed a gentle, nibbling kiss on the spot she pointed to, anyway. Then he blew a soft raspberry on her wrist until she giggled and kicked in his arms.

"Da," she protested, laughing and twisting her fingers into his hair as he continued to blow on her arm.

When he raised his head, Rachel was looking at him, her eyes soft and...sad?

"Janey's all right," he assured her. "I think I scared her more than hurt her."

At that, Rachel turned her back on him. "As if I think that you'd ever *intentionally* hurt anyone, Sam," she said, lowering Zach to the sidewalk next to the van.

Intentionally? She had stressed the word.

And in Sam's mind he saw a laughing, zestful Rachel rushing in the door with his sister, Kate. He saw a shadow of that same girl slipping out the door only a week later when he came home. What had happened? Or rather, what was it he had done? He'd always worried that some terrible part of her home life had been transferred over to him, but now—he'd done something. He couldn't escape the conviction that he *had* done something to this gentle lady.

"Rachel," he said softly, hoping she'd turn around. "I would never have hurt you intentionally, either. You were the sweetest kid I'd ever met. Whatever it was, whatever I did, I'm sorry."

Rachel blindly slid her fingers along the side of the van, fumbling for the door handle. The sweetest *kid*. Maybe that had hurt more than the pity part. He had thought her a child back then, while she had been spinning romantic fantasies. And of course she *had* been barely out of childhood. But it wasn't the word alone. It was what the word *kid* implied. When he'd said it years ago, when he'd told Donna to stop spinning gossip about the "poor, needy kid," Rachel had known all her fantasies were just that.

She'd realized that Sam wasn't going to love her—ever. He hadn't thought of her "that way," just as she didn't think of Bob Engalls as more than a very nice man. And it had hurt to realize that.

Striving for control, Rachel realized that it still hurt. Even more, now that she'd grown up and gotten to know him, now that she'd moved into his world. But none of that had ever been his fault. Not then. Not now. She couldn't blame the man for what he'd never been able to feel for her—and she certainly couldn't bare her soul to him now any more than she could have then. The fact was that she had already made a decision about today, and she was damned determined not to spoil things this time with regrets or embarrassing explanations. Pasting on her smile, she yanked on the door and fastened Zach in his car seat before turning back to Sam.

"Sam," she said, shaking her head. "I *was* a foolish kid. The reason I spent so much time out of sorts with you—well, it doesn't even matter now. Let's forget it, okay? Today's a new day, a great day to be out in the sun with the kids. Let's whoop it up and pretend all that stuff never happened, all right?"

She could see by the darkening of Sam's eyes, the tightening of his jaw, that he didn't want to let this subject drop. Now that she'd foolishly admitted that something *had* happened years ago, he didn't want to let it go. He was determined to dig out all the details and make right something that Rachel knew couldn't be made right.

Opening her mouth to speak, she shook her head. "Don't push it, Sam," she said.

"Haven't I always?" His voice was low and coaxing.

She jerked her head up, surprised. "No," she answered softly. "You were always a perfect gentleman even when I didn't deserve it." But a vision of herself leaning back over Sam's arm just a week earlier pushed into Rachel's mind. Maybe not a *perfect* gentleman. She could feel the flush climbing up her throat.

Apparently Sam could see her discomposure, too. He blew out a long, frustrated breath.

"Okay, you win this time, Rachel," he agreed, moving up to lift Janey into her place beside Zach. "But someday, someday, sweet lady, you and I are going to sit down and you're going to spill all your secrets to me. I mean to know what I did to you and make up for it somehow."

Slow panic began to rise in Rachel, but she refused to let it show. "Oh?" she asked, raising a brow. "And how do you intend to make me talk, Sam?"

He cocked one brow. "Simple. Bribery," he said with a slow grin.

"More flowers?" she asked incredulously.

Sam shook his head. "No, somehow I don't think even flowers would be enough, Rachel. You hold your secrets pretty close. But—darn it, lady. Why won't you tell me?" He slammed his hand against the van, then laughed. "Guess I'm being pretty overbearing, aren't I?"

Rachel smiled at his crestfallen look. "That's okay, Sam. You can be overbearing as long as I can remain a woman of mystery, all right?"

"A woman of mystery?"

"All right, a royal pain in the backside," she agreed. "Let's just go home, Sam."

At her slip of the tongue, Rachel caught her breath, but Sam seemed to see nothing wrong with her calling *his* house *home*.

"All right, Rachel," he said, catching Annie up as she headed their way, tumbling toward him. "But I hope that someday you'll change your mind. Maybe you'll trust me with those secrets, and we'll clear all this up."

Maybe. And maybe Santa Claus would come to town in July, Rachel thought. Because much as she wanted to be upfront with Sam, there was no way she could explain what he wanted to know. She couldn't tell him that she'd once been hurt because she loved him—because then he'd wonder—did she love him still?

And that was a question Rachel couldn't answer. It was a question she didn't even want to face herself.

Don would be here soon, and then she'd see. She'd see if things had changed.

Sam rested his arms on the now still Rototiller. He surveyed his property, the sun beating a path through the treetops and dappling everything with golden light. It was amazing what one tenacious, determined woman could do, he marveled, looking at the landscape before him. The big white Victorian was brightly accessorized, the corners flanked by full-leafed lilac bushes that would bring fragrance and color to his house next year. The old roses that had been struggling to survive were cleared of the choking weeds, budding, ready to pop out in shades of deepest red and purest white. Plots of yellow marigolds, blue ageratum, and scarlet geraniums lent a bold dash of color. But of all the additions to this house, the most precious of all was the group of people down on their hands and knees at the base of the last lilac bush.

Rachel crouched there with his children, pointing to something in the dirt.

"It's a cicada's shell," she explained. "They only come out every seventeen years, but now and then you can still find one of their shells underground."

"Seventeen years?" Annie echoed.

"Yes, angel." Rachel nodded, smiling into the little girl's eyes. "You'll be almost grown up by the next time they come around. And it's something to see, I'll tell you. Lots and lots of cicadas, all responding to nature's timetable and then disappearing for another seventeen years."

"You've seen them?" Annie asked as Janey and Zach sat down, more interested in the small plastic shovels Rachel had given them. Janey picked up a teaspoon's worth of dirt and tossed it in the air.

"Yeah?" her friend Nicky asked, clearly awestruck at Rachel's announcement.

"Definitely," Rachel agreed with a smile.

"Wow, you must be really old," Nicky said.

Annie nodded, big-eyed. "If you remember something that only happens every seventeen years, you *must* be old, Rachel," she agreed.

"Old?" Rachel's laugh trilled over the yard. "Old, am I? Bet I can beat you to the maple tree in the front of the house," she challenged. "And I'll give you a five-second lead, okay?"

At that, the two little girls shrieked and began to run, giggling all the way. As Sam watched Annie's little feet pound over the grass, he noticed that Rachel gave them way more than a five-second lead. He heard her as she called, "Keep your eye on Janey and Zach, Sam, okay? I'll be right back."

Then she took off in a streak, her slender legs a flash of pale, shapely flesh, her long hair streaming out behind her. She was life itself—bright and beautiful and oh, so alluring. When she rounded the house, chasing the squealing, excited little girls, it was as if she carried the sun beneath her arm.

Without a thought, Sam strolled over to Janey and Zach, scooping them into his arms with a big hug and kiss.

"Come on, you two, we're missing all the fun," he confided with a grin.

"Some?" Zach asked, holding up his shovel.

"You little squirt, are you eating that stuff?" he asked, peering at his son's mouth.

"No," Zach said solemnly. "No, no, no." It was clear that someone had already warned him against the dangers of eating dirt. Sam should have known that Rachel would already be wise to the lure of a good spoonful of soil. After all, she'd practically raised the Allyn clan. She'd known all the ins and outs of kids.

Even so, as he turned the corner and found Rachel, Nicky and Annie, all propped against the oak tree, his heart still gave a lurch at what he saw there, at what he should have expected. Annie was smiling, her mouth tilted up so wide her dimples had returned.

"I won, Daddy. I won the race, even though Rachel and Nicky ran very fast. Rachel almost won, she almost did, but I passed her just at the last second."

Stepping close, Sam noted Nicky's short little legs, legs not made for running races. But Rachel's were long. Achingly long, he noted. His daughter was no runner, but still she had won against a long-legged gazelle of a woman.

And Annie was excited, tremendously excited, so much so that the dark cast that had lived in her eyes for a year was missing at the moment.

As he opened his mouth to speak, Rachel stepped into his space, close enough to make his heart trip and speed up. "Annie won," she whispered, as if he was going to argue, before she hurriedly retreated back to her place against the tree.

"Don't worry, Rachel," Annie said, tugging at Rachel's fingers. "You were prob'ly just tired from all that work. Rachel has seen bugs that only come around every seventeen years," she confided to her father.

"We better not let her overdo things, then," Sam said, quirking up one corner of his mouth as he tried not to laugh. "Anyone who's lived that long should probably rest after a big race. Why don't you and Nicky play for a while and I'll put the twins down for a nap in a few minutes? I think they've eaten enough dirt for one day."

Rachel automatically looked at the shovels Zach and Janey were dangling. Zach frowned at his daddy. "No," he said, in a voice as stern as an eighteen-month-old could manage.

"Looks like you taught them well," Sam confided as Rachel relaxed and wrinkled her nose at his teasing grin. "I almost had you going," he confided, lowering his voice as he moved closer. Letting the twins slide down to play in the soft grass at the base of the tree, Sam took one step farther in.

He was standing a step away from Rachel now, whisper close, and he knew he shouldn't be there, but she was like a lure, impossibly enticing. Her hair had been pushed back, exposing the long, curving line of her neck where moisture beaded and ran down into the shadows beneath her blouse. Sam had a sudden urge to lean forward and trace his lips down her throat to the catch on her blouse and below. If they'd been alone...well, thank goodness they weren't alone. But still, he didn't bother stepping away.

He turned and felt her hair catch on his sleeve.

Rachel swallowed. He saw the pulse beating in her throat.

"I—I guess I'll be going then. Sleep tight, sweethearts," she said to Janey and Zach. "You and Nicky enjoy the day," she told Annie.

Don't go, Sam wanted to say, but he didn't. What would his excuse be? That he wanted to look at her, to touch her?

"Don't go," Annie said. "Please stay longer, Rachel. Stay for dinner. Daddy and I will cook, won't we, Daddy? You won't even have to work. It's Saturday. There's still lots of time. You can sit out on the porch and rest and drink lemonade. Don't go just yet." And moving toward her father and Rachel, Annie grasped Rachel's hand. She looked up into the lovely lady's eyes. The eyes of the woman who'd let his child win a race. He wondered if Annie knew...or even if she cared. Whatever, it was clear as Annie's eyes that she didn't want Rachel to go home yet. It was obvious that Annie had accepted this woman into her heart.

He could see the slight tremble of Rachel's lips as his child grasped her hand and made her plea. He felt the moment Rachel turned her gaze to his. He was almost afraid to look and he wasn't sure why. Like Annie, he wanted Rachel to stay longer. She was a woman who had changed his daughter's life. She was also the woman who made him get the shakes whenever he got too close. He knew without a doubt that he wanted this woman, knew all too well that was a danger. Wanting her, desiring her. He should probably be hoping that she'd remember some sensible errand she had and leave. But she wouldn't do that. Sam knew it. If the president of the United States was calling her to Washington right now, she'd tell him she couldn't come.

She'd stay because a child needed her, but he wondered what she'd say if he told her that there was a man who wanted her. And he *did* want her. Badly. Wanted his lips against her soft, sweet flesh, his hands skimming over her hips.

Standing there, staring into her eyes, Sam tried to tamp down his desire. Still, he saw Rachel's breath catch. Quickly she looked down at Annie and managed a shaky smile.

"Does that mean we'll be having hot dogs? Wasn't that the only thing your daddy could cook?"

Annie bit her lip. "Does it matter?"

"No." Rachel shook her head. "It's a good day for hot dogs, sweetheart. A perfect day."

But as she silently took a snoozy Janey and Zach from him, as she walked away and he watched the gentle sway of her hips as she strode up the stairs to the porch, it wasn't hot dogs Sam had on his mind.

It was Rachel. She walked across that porch, looking like she belonged there. In his house. With his kids. In his bed.

As the door closed behind her, Sam could still see her standing against that tree. Dark hair and creamy skin, a wood nymph made of flesh and bone, her woman scent curling around and drifting into his consciousness. Alluring, maddening, the way she made him burn, the way she fit in so effortlessly. She touched his children, his home, and turned things bright and beautiful. Only he was left wanting, untouched . . . and he very much wished for Rachel to touch him. He craved the freedom to touch back.

It was a danger, a real danger—and yet not a danger at all this time, this hunger for her. *This* time he wasn't talking about love, he wasn't talking about the kind of relationship he'd had with Donna.

He was talking about a woman who fit. A woman who fit his home, his kids, his body. That was all.

This was safer, this was better, this was the way things should be. The only problem was—would Rachel see things in the same light?

Hell, Sam thought, standing alone now beneath the tree. If he was stupid enough to tell Rachel he wanted her in his bed, he'd be lucky if he escaped with his head on his body.

Standing inside the house after she'd put the twins to bed, Rachel leaned against the door, breathing hard, trying to make sense of her thoughts.

For a while there, with Sam nearly pressed against her side, she'd been almost unable to function. Only the presence of the children and the knowledge that she was in danger of making a fool of herself once again had kept her coherent.

And now she had agreed to stick around longer, to stay, when she wanted nothing more than to speed away and not look back.

"So what are you going to do, Rachel?" she muttered, remembering the look on Annie's face, the pleading in her eyes. She could no more have walked away tonight than she could have stopped the greening of the earth—or the devastating smile that touched Sam's face so often.

Darn! Couldn't she get that man out of her mind for more than five minutes?

Determined to do just that, Rachel pushed off the door and made her way to the kitchen. From here, she could get something done and feel useful, not just flustered.

She could also look out the window and see Sam adjusting the tilt of the tire swing he had hung from a sturdy oak at the edge of his property. She could see him lifting the little girls into the swing and see him pushing it in swaying circles as Nicky and Annie held their heads back, letting their hair billow out behind them. She could hear the interplay of little girls giggling, begging for just one more push while the man answered in that low, sandy voice of his, readily agreeing to their childish demands.

No, it seemed she couldn't get away from Sam, not in her thoughts or anywhere else in her life.

Humph. Rachel reached out and pulled the shade down over the window. Immediately the glow of the sun disappeared, the sound of the delighted voices outside muted. She was cocooned in here, hiding from the light and the love outside. Rachel knew that, but heavens, what else could she do?

She could occupy her mind and her hands. And digging through the pantry and the cabinets, Rachel set out to do that. She dug out pots and pans and food. She dragged an ancient cookbook from its space on the counter. She thumbed through its pages, finally, finally losing herself to her task.

"What in heaven's name are you doing, lady?"

The deep, masculine voice behind her caught her off guard and Rachel whirled around, dropping the muffin tin she held in her hands. It clattered against the linoleum.

For three seconds, maybe four, there was silence as Sam and Rachel stood there staring at each other across the broad expanse of white vinyl floor that separated them. Watching the man, knowing just how foolish she was for even being here, wondering if she was staying just for Annie or partly for herself, Rachel swallowed. She opened her mouth, closed it again, closed her eyes.

"Rachel." Sam's voice turned soft and soothing, melting with regret. "God, Rachel, I'm sorry. I didn't mean to startle you so."

He came up close beside her then, reached down, and picked up the tin. When he placed it in her hand, she wondered if he could feel her fingers shaking as she tried to grasp the cool metal. She wondered *why* her fingers were shaking. As he said, she'd been startled, but that was all. There was no reason she should be losing control—except that Sam was touching her again.

"I'm—all right, thank you," she said as Sam backed away, giving her breathing space. "What—what are the girls doing?"

His smile was automatic, easy once again. "They're riding bikes, they're running, they're playing hide-and-seek, being kids. Just—being kids."

To anyone else, that might have seemed like an ordinary statement, but Rachel knew that to Sam it was not. He'd told her that Annie hadn't acted like a child in a long while. She'd seen for herself that it was so. But today...

"I'm so glad to hear that," she said, and she was. "Annie's very special to me."

"You let her win the race," he said accusingly, drawing near again, giving her that direct, blue-eyed stare that made her feel like she was desert-dry tinder ready to flicker into flame before him.

"No, I didn't," she said, shaking her head insistently. "I knew you'd think so, but I really didn't. It would have been cheating, she would have known."

Sam crossed his arms, he raised his brows in disbelief. "You've got legs like a baby giraffe, sweetheart. A lot more shapely, of course," he continued when she started to open her mouth. "But still, you've got mile-high legs. And of course, you gave her at least a ten-second lead to a tree that was right around the corner."

"Well," Rachel said, laughing and lowering her voice in case the girls were anywhere near. "She still won fair and square. That little darling of yours really put the pedal to the metal at the end, so, the extra few seconds..." She raised one shoulder in a helpless shrug. "They didn't really matter. What mattered was that she was really trying. She really wanted to win, to do something badly for the first time in a long time. She was incredible. *Is* incredible," she corrected herself.

Giving up, Sam held out his hands in a gesture of defeat. "And you, lady, are pretty incredible, too. What the hell do you think you're doing in here rummaging through all this rubble? Step aside, please. Didn't Annie tell you that the Graysons were providing dinner tonight?"

"I know, but..."

"But nothing. Just move that gorgeous little behind of yours, lady, or else I'll move it for you. I intend to show you what Sam Grayson can do with a few friendly appliances."

The sexy teasing note in Sam's voice had Rachel smiling all over again, feeling calmer, safe from her own emotions once again. Nevertheless, when he moved to remove her from her place by the counter, she gave a small shriek and feinted to the left.

"Okay, you win, Sam," she agreed, laughing. "Bring on the hot dogs."

Sam paused, his hands on his hips.

"Aw, Rachel, you wound me. I realize that you have it on good authority that I am a lousy cook, but hey, I don't wear that Stetson for nothing, you know. My roots are in Texas, and I can grill a steak with the best of the boys. So you just sit yourself down and rest while I rustle up some grub."

She nodded. "All right. But I could make a salad."

Sam's brows drew together in a mock-threatening frown. "And you could find yourself carried outside and dumped on the porch swing, too. You've done enough for today, Rachel. It's supposed to be your weekend. So rest, lady. Take it easy, put your feet up. You've worked your miracle for the day with Annie. Now lean back and let me take over from here."

"You're sure? I could—"

"Rachel?" Sam's voice was soft, soothing, mesmerizing.

"Yes?"

"Shut those beautiful lips, Rachel. Now, please."

He was staring at her mouth, his eyes dark and harassed. Her lips tingled, and she raised her fingers. Halfway there, she stopped, hoping he hadn't seen her gesture.

"I'll just go outside," she agreed. "But Sam?"

He looked up.

"Call me if you need me."

"Go." His voice was strangled. He looked like a man capable of anything, cooking a steak, or kissing a woman senseless to shut her up.

Rachel scooted out the door.

A short hour later she was in steak heaven, her lips moist with the juices of the wonderful T-bone that Sam had prepared.

Outside on the lawn, Sam had gathered his little clan. He'd called Cynthia and gotten permission for Nicky to stay a while longer. They'd feasted on steak and baked potatoes, salad and light-as-air biscuits.

At Rachel's questioning stare, Sam shrugged.

"My mother insisted I be able to cook at least one decent meal. I guess she was afraid that no woman would want me and I'd starve to death."

But of course, Rachel remembered, that had been a joke. Girls had crowded around Sam in droves. He had loved and married young. Now he was back, come full circle, a confirmed bachelor who'd written the possibility of love out of his life.

That was why he allowed her here. Because she was no threat, because he didn't view her as a possible source of love or betrayal.

The thought snuck in, hit Rachel below the belt. Suddenly she wasn't hungry. She wanted to be up and away from her thoughts.

Quickly she bent to gather up the dishes and the blanket, all that was left after the girls had run off to catch fireflies.

When Sam moved to help her, she shook her head. Hard.

"I'll just stack the dishes in the dishwasher and come back with a couple of jars. That's all. They can catch fireflies, and we'll let them go in a little while. It's what kids do on a summer night. Remember?"

"One of the best parts of summer, Rachel. I remember it all. I remember helping you and Kate when you were old enough to have lost the thrill for a good firefly chase, but you didn't, did you? You never lost that glow."

Rachel turned to look at Sam. In the gathering darkness she could just make out his outline, but as she made her escape, she was sure he was watching her. His gaze was like a soft stroke down her spine, a long, slow caress. She could escape Sam, but she couldn't escape from whatever it was that happened between them whenever he looked at her, whenever he touched her.

Desire. Thick and hot and demanding.

Sam wanted her.

She wanted him back. But . . .

Rachel pressed on into the house. She clamped down on her thoughts, she forced herself to think only of the magic of the night, of the children, of the joy of catching the season's first fireflies.

And Sam let her forget—for a while. Like a kid himself, he gently caught the bright insects, held them close for the twins to see, then sent them winging on their way into the night.

"Bug," Janey said, satisfied, when Sam had caught another.

"Bug," Zach agreed on a yawn.

"Yes, bug," Sam said. "But now it's bedtime, I think. Come on, let's go," he said, taking a toddling child on either hand.

Rachel watched them go. And while Sam corralled his babies off to see the sandman, she trundled Nicky into Cynthia's car. Then she escorted a swaying Annie in and stayed close as the child brushed her teeth and got ready for bed.

"Sleep tight, speed demon," she said, kissing Annie on the forehead and tucking her into bed. "I'll send your daddy to you in a minute," she promised.

Annie nodded and pulled Rachel down for one last hug. "This was fun, Rachel. Come catch fireflies with us again, okay?"

Fortunately Annie was too far gone to expect an answer. Passing Sam in the hallway as she left, Rachel meant just to peep in on the twins, then slip out in the darkness back to her house.

"Stay just a minute," Sam whispered as he brushed against her in the cramped hallway.

Rachel looked up to where Sam's face should be. Somehow, not seeing him, she was even more aware of his presence, of the sound of his voice, the warmth flowing from his body to hers.

"I should go," she managed to say, her voice barely making it past her lips.

"I know," he agreed. "But don't. Not just yet. I need to talk to you for a minute."

And Rachel nodded, knowing Sam couldn't see her, but unable to say yes when she knew she should say no.

Chapter Eight

What in hell was he doing?

Sam could feel the anxiety rolling off of Rachel, he knew he should let her go. But his mind had been spinning all day long, ever since she first called him. His gut had started churning every time she came near.

She was driving him certifiably insane. Everything she did, every time she moved. He hadn't felt this way in a long time. No, he hadn't ever felt desire that slipped beneath his defenses the way it did with Rachel. And just now, knowing she had come from his daughter's room, hearing the soft whispered exchange as he moved out into the hallway... had left him with a feeling of... right.

Now, moving back out into the shadowed hallway after kissing an already sleeping Annie good-night, he followed the scent of Rachel, down the stairs, out the door, onto the porch. Softly scented lemons. Soap. Woman. He wanted to drink it in, run his fingers through that long hair of hers, bury his face in its softness and scent.

Instead he simply stepped out onto the unlit porch.

She turned, waiting for whatever he had to say.

And what could he say? *I want you? You're driving me crazy with lust? I need you now, Rachel?*

"Come here," he simply said, although it was he who took the steps that brought him to the lady's side. And he was the one who opened his mouth to speak and found himself wordless.

"What is it, Sam?" Rachel asked, and her voice was trembling. Had he scared her? Oh, damn him for a worthless idiot if he'd done that.

"Rachel. Rachel, you amaze me, astound me. Completely," he simply said. "I come into town, practically order you to my house, I assault you with flowers day after day, batter your defenses, and yet you come. You stay. You make my children sleep soundly at night."

A soft sigh escaped her lips. In the moonlight he watched her drop her head forward as if she'd been waiting for something else, something more ominous.

"Oh, Sam," she said on a breath. That was it. Just *Oh, Sam.*

It was all he needed, all he wanted. Slipping his hands beneath her hair, he framed her skull with his palms, waiting for her to turn her face up to his.

She did. Slowly she lifted her head. The moonlight sparkled across her eyes, and he saw the need written there. Need he recognized because he felt it, too.

Marry me, Rachel. The words slipped into his consciousness, echoed around his brain, but he refused to let them take shape. He knew the dangers of jumping in like that, he knew better than to get carried away, knew this woman had turned down other men.

Marry me. But it wasn't marriage he wanted, he told himself, pulling her close as he brought his lips down on top of hers. It was just her. Just Rachel.

Marry me. The words sounded more right with each beat of his heart. They drove into his soul as he drank the nectar from within her, rubbed his lips against hers, nibbling, sucking, tasting her.

She kissed him back, her body pressing up against his as a strangled cry escaped her.

Gathering her closer, trying to bring her into his body, he half lifted her off the ground, he took her weight, the soft velvet warmth of her. He felt her body mold itself to his.

"Rachel. Oh, lady, I want you."

A groan escaped him; he felt a shiver run through her. Then, as his words died away, as though she'd just realized what he was saying, Rachel pushed back, still within the circle of his arms.

"Sam." His name was a moan on her lips. "I can't, Sam."

Her mouth was a heartbeat away from his, still close but retreating. If he'd wanted to, he could have forced her back to him, but he'd never do that. She had to come to him willingly.

Staring down into her lovely gray eyes, Sam fought his desire. He swallowed hard, then purposefully set her away from him. She was sweet honey, warm skin, cream that could make a man lick his lips and ask for more. She was everything he wanted tonight—but others had wanted her, too. And she'd said no. She was saying no now. He couldn't push her any further and still live with himself the next day.

Silently he let her go, felt her slide down his body until her feet touched the wooden floorboards. She stepped back and away.

Now his hands felt empty, his body too cool, his heart—damn! He braced a palm against the chain of the porch swing and blew out a long sigh.

"You've never married," he said simply. "But you're a natural with children. You're a damned desirable woman. It's none of my business. Slap me for asking if you want to, but...why?"

"Why haven't I married?" Her words were a whisper brushing past him.

As he turned to her, she looked away, for once unwilling to meet his gaze.

"I suppose I've just never found what I've been looking for," she said softly.

Sam felt the blow like an arrow piercing his body. "And what's that?" He said the words so casually, yet deep inside he knew they were important. Too damned important.

She turned to him then, meeting his gaze directly. "Someone I loved. Someone who loved me back. Desire's not enough, Sam."

And she'd been desired. He knew that just as sure as he knew his own name. Men had wanted her, had made her offers, but she'd turned them down, every one. She was waiting for the right man, the only man...and she hadn't found him.

The arrow slid in a few inches deeper, hitting nerve, muscle, bone, striking hard. He shouldn't have touched her. It had not made things better, had only buried her deeper in his soul. And she was standing there, looking wounded, raw, uncertain, probably upset that she'd let her desire for him show as well. At least she hadn't denied that she wanted him. She hadn't said that.

Well, he was the one who started this mess. He would make sure that he ended it right. He wouldn't have her lying awake, worrying about this moment.

Moving away from the swing, he stepped forward, sliding his palm up her cheek, brushing her lips softly once again.

"I won't say that I'm sorry I kissed you this time, Rachel. When I said I wanted you, I meant it, and it would be a lie to deny it, one you'd recognize. There's something about you, something that makes my blood run hot and fast... but I promise you this much. I'll do my best to control it. That doesn't mean you won't have to remind me again not to push things. It doesn't mean I'll stop wanting you, but—don't let this be a wall between us. Don't let that happen."

He stood there staring down at her, wondering what she was thinking, if she was hating him for putting her in this unthinkable position. He would never know, because she wouldn't walk away, at least not while his children were still in her care.

Her nod was quick and silent. Relief flooded through him like an overflowing river.

"Shall we start again?" he asked finally, striving for lightness that didn't come. "Friends?" He forced the word past his teeth.

She stood there barely breathing, nodding hard before she spun around and practically tripped down the steps, barreling toward her car.

"Friends," he thought he heard her call softly, just before she drove off into the night.

Long after she'd gone, Sam stood there, staring out into the clear, dark sky. *Friends.* Why had he said it? It was a fine word, a good word, but it in no way described what he felt toward Rachel. On the other hand, their path had been made clear tonight. She wanted him, he wanted her, but it was just not going to happen. If they were friends, if he could make that leap... maybe it would make things that much easier when she finally did meet the right man. Maybe then he would be able to smile as she walked down the aisle to another man. The right man.

Maybe if he said the word often enough, he would stop wanting her someday.

But not yet, Sam thought as he lay back in bed and longed for the woman who would never be his. Not tonight.

Leaning over Zach's crib several days later, Rachel soothed one hand over the little boy's fluffy baby curls. He stared up at her, his big brown eyes absolutely trusting as he smacked his lips in her direction.

"Sleep tight, angel," she said as she bent to brush her lips against the softness of his cheek.

"Seep," he agreed, but when she meant to move away, he wound his little arms around her neck. For a few seconds the scent of baby powder drifted around her. The feel of feather-soft skin and a tiny heartbeat fluttering beneath her chin nearly undid Rachel. Maybe Zach was only following Janey's lead in hugging her, but whatever the reasons, this tiny boy and that sweet munchkin already snoozing in the next crib over had crawled into her heart.

She'd already fallen in love with them, would fight for them, give her own life to save theirs if necessary...and it seemed they were beginning to get used to her, too.

Untangling herself from Zach's relaxed grasp, Rachel kissed her fingertips and soothed them over his forehead, down his nose, causing his already sagging eyelids to close completely.

"Goodnight, sweetheart," she whispered, though she knew he was drifting off, almost beyond hearing.

The words caught, clogged her throat. She was in deep, way too deep. She'd known it the other night when she'd been lost in Sam's arms. She'd tried to run from it, when he'd accepted her denial of his caresses and so easily turned from lover to friend.

Rachel knew what Sam was looking for... and it wasn't her sharing his life. He'd made that clear, hadn't bothered lying. He wanted someone he could trust to care for his children above all else... but he was also flesh and blood and bone. It was only natural that, spending as much time as they did together, there would be passion between them. If she would be baby-sitter and woman as well, if she'd been willing— Dear heaven, she *had* been willing. She'd ached to give in to the temptation of having Sam's hands and lips on her body. She'd wanted the freedom to allow her own lips to roam. But... she couldn't have handled it, wouldn't have been able to control it. Sam would have known that for her there was nothing casual about touching and being touched by him. And while Sam would willingly give her pleasure, and he would offer her friendship... his heart was unavailable.

This was not, nor would it ever be, a permanent arrangement. Someday she'd have to go.

Remembering Zach and Janey's hugs, Annie's wounded eyes, Rachel knew it would have to be soon. She had to be careful. So very careful. She wouldn't hurt her babies for the world. She couldn't bear to leave them thinking that she didn't care enough to stay... when in fact, she cared too much. Just too damn much.

Closing the door behind her, Rachel wandered out on the landing, started down the stairs... and found Sam staring up at her.

Her hand clenched on the railing.

"I—I didn't know it was so late," she stammered as he continued to gaze up at her. Standing there, poised above him like a woman on a pedestal, her loose blouse suddenly felt too tight, too seductive, when in fact it was only her usual, white cotton with a modest vee neckline. She tugged at the leg of her cutoff shorts, stilling her hand when he turned his attention to the point where thigh met blue denim.

Sam dragged his gaze away from Rachel's legs and up to her wide, distressed, gray eyes.

"It's not late," he admitted. "I came home a little early tonight." But why? He hoped she didn't ask that question because he damn well wasn't sure he could answer it himself. Because days had passed and he wanted to see if time had helped? Because he needed to know if he could really ignore the disastrous things Rachel did to his insides and step into the role of *friend, pal?*

Nice try, Grayson, he thought, noticing the slight tremble in her lips. It would have been crystal clear to a monkey that he wasn't going to be able to sling a careless arm around Rachel's shoulder and proclaim her his buddy. The woman did things to white cotton that he would never have imagined if he hadn't seen it firsthand. What's more, with that hand clenching the railing so hard, with those eyes looking dark and pained, he wanted nothing more than to wrap her up and protect her from whatever idiot had caused her grief. In this case, he suspected, that idiot would be himself. He was the one, after all, who had claimed to hire her to care for his children and then practically licked his way down her body in full view of anyone who cared to drive past his front porch.

Fool.

"Where are my little monsters?" he asked, determined to let her know that things were different tonight. He was in control of his baser instincts.

She smiled at his teasing tone, and Sam's heart started pounding. He ignored it.

"The little monsters?" she asked. "They're snoozing peacefully, and you darn well know that they're as angelic as babies only a few months away from the 'terrible twos' can be. And Annie, she's with Nicky, and Michelle Wilkins. She'll be home soon. I was just going to start dinner." She continued down the stairs, obviously intent on getting to her tasks.

Sam stopped her by holding out one hand. His fingers were mere inches from her arm, but he didn't touch. He didn't trust himself to get near even something as innocuous as her wrist.

"Wait. I've got something to tell you."

Rachel bit her lip, then nodded quickly. "All right, why don't we go outside. I have a few things to talk to you about, as well. We'll watch for Annie."

Her expression was filled with meaning. It was clear that she didn't want Annie to sneak in and hear this conversation. What were those "things" she wanted to talk to him about? Sam sucked in air, wondering why he felt as if a mountain was about to tumble onto his head.

For the last few days, every time he went into town, each day at work, the talk seemed to center around Don Bowers and what was going to happen when the man came back into town. The money was running on the man's success. People were saying that Rachel had been too grief-stricken to know her own mind when he was in town last. They were asking questions the way people do. Was Rachel going to marry the man? Was she going to leave Tucker? Was she going to discover that she really was in love after all with the guy who'd waited for her and given her the gift of time?

Sam tried to ignore the red-hot sliver of pain that snaked down into his chest and curled around his heart, squeezing hard. He gave a tight nod, holding the door open for Rachel. When she walked past him, the desire to reach out and touch was overwhelming. He squeezed the doorknob hard, wondering if the imprint of his fingers would still be here when his grandchildren were running around the place.

"What is it you wanted to talk about?" he managed to ask, his voice coming out too gravelly, too rough. Maybe she'd heard all the talk; surely she had. Maybe she wanted to prepare him for the fact that she wanted out. If she loved that guy... oh, damn, could he persuade her to stay?

No. She'd given him so much, she'd brought life back into his household. He couldn't cheat her out of what she wanted, of what she absolutely deserved.

Sam cleared his throat, preparing himself to talk about something he didn't even want to think about. He stared off in the distance, watching his daughter and her two young friends work their way up the limbs of a tree on the outskirts of his lot.

"Look at them, will you?" he asked, fierce pride and an unwillingness to jump into the topic of Don Bowers leading him to stop her answer to his question. "They look like they're having the time of their lives."

The floorboards creaked lightly beside him. "I know," Rachel agreed, "and I'm glad Annie found some friends right away. I'm sure she still misses her mother now and then, but Nicky and Michelle make her forget a great deal of the time, I think."

Sam looked at the three children, so different in physical appearance. Annie, a tiny little fairy of a girl; Nicky, short and round; and Michelle, skinny and tall as a cattail. Her ragged jeans were at least two inches too short for her lengthy frame.

Sighing, Sam turned to Rachel. "I'm glad, too. I just wish there was something I could do to help Michelle. Her dad works down at the yard, but I suspect he drinks up half his pay. She and her sisters barely have food and clothing to get them through the week."

Rachel turned suddenly, her expression unreadable.

"She seems happy enough." Her voice was slightly chilled.

Sam lifted one shoulder. "Happy doesn't pay the bills."

Turning aside, Rachel's jaw was tight and tense. "No, it doesn't. You pity her, then?"

Her voice was not much more than a wisp of sound. Her shoulders were rigid, her whole body tight, waiting. Sam was free to study her, turned away as she was. He remembered another long-legged child, running with the wind. A child whose eyes could glow bright as stars... once upon a time.

"*Pity* isn't the word for a child like that," he whispered. "How can anyone pity a kid who doesn't know that the sun shines for everyone, not especially for her? How could I feel sorry for someone who has so much life in her that it practically spills over with every step she takes?"

"She's needy, she's poverty-stricken," Rachel reminded him.

"Damn right she is, and for that I want to help her. I'd like to fire her daddy, but what good would that do? Then there'd be *no* money coming her way. I want to help, but I don't know how. I'm just glad that she and Annie have become friends. I can at least give her a decent meal now and then."

Without allowing himself time to think, he reached out and took Rachel by the elbows, turned her to face him directly. "It's all right to do that much, isn't it, Rachel?"

Sam wasn't even sure what he was asking, but he knew for certain that it was tied somehow to a much younger Rachel, a much younger Sam.

She nodded, staring into his eyes. The breeze picked up a lock of her hair, tossing it forward against his neck. They were joined, they would *never* be joined, but on this, Sam suspected, it was important that they at least agree.

"It's more than all right to do that much, Sam. Just don't ever make her feel that you're doing it out of pity, all right?"

He knew for sure now that they were talking about more than Michelle Wilkins. He opened his mouth to speak, but Rachel placed her fingers upon his lips.

"There's something important that I want to talk to you about, Sam."

Her voice was strained. He waited, the light touch of her fingers holding him immobile.

"I wanted to talk to you about Annie," Rachel said, stepping back, now that he was silent. "And Janey and Zach. They're so...special. You must be so proud of them, Sam. They give the word *sweet* a whole new meaning. And I—I suppose that's why I'm worried about them. That's what I wanted to talk to you about."

Sam stared down at her, trying to read her expression. Her arms were crossed over her chest protectively. She was chewing her lip nervously. So it wasn't Don Bowers she had wanted to talk about. She wasn't discussing marriage to the man, at least not today. Rachel was worried, plainly worried.

He tipped her chin up with his finger, met her gaze.

"You think my children are too sweet?" he asked incredulously, knowing, of course, that wasn't the point at all.

"I think they can be easily hurt," she admitted with a nod. "And I know—*you* know, that Annie can. It wouldn't do for them to become too attached to me. I wouldn't want to ever run the risk of hurting them in any way, even if it was unintentional."

Her eyes were dark, the gray of a cloudy sky just before the rain.

She *was* thinking of leaving. *Seriously* thinking of going. That man. He was coming for her, she was waiting for him. But it was killing her to think that she could ever hurt a child.

Sam reached out and slid one hand along her jaw. He stroked his thumb across her cheek. She was worried for his children's sake, and suddenly Sam was just as worried for Rachel.

How had he complicated her life? She hadn't asked for all this. He'd pushed it on her, and now—aw hell, he'd known all along that she was more warmhearted than other women. He'd realized that, even in the early days when he was still living with his resentment of Donna's deception, of Rachel's dismissal of him. And now she was aching inside—because his manipulating ways had forced her to do something she'd never do under normal circumstances: bring possible pain to an innocent. And Sam knew full well that she would shield his babies, save them as much as possible, even at a cost to herself.

She was leaving soon. He wanted to swear. He wanted to kick something so hard that the physical pain would dull the tripping of his heart. "I didn't mean to involve you this much," he said gently.

"Don't you think I know that? But now, if—"

She held her hands out helplessly.

Sam heard the strain in her voice. He should be trying to make this easier for her. But dammit, he couldn't. That was one thing he couldn't do.

Marry me. The words filled his mind. He pushed them away. He was a simple man, a man whose life revolved around his children and his work. He didn't know how to keep a woman happy, not enough to make her stay, not enough to make sure she wouldn't turn away from him when he was least expecting it. Didn't he remember that? It had happened with Donna. It had already happened once with Rachel.

Marry me. He sucked in air, ignoring his thoughts as best he could.

"Rachel." He reached out, touched her lips with his thumb. "You don't have to leave. I'll keep my hands to myself. We can work things out."

It took a mammoth effort for him to manage an encouraging smile, especially when it felt like there was a steamroller parked on his chest, but he did it. He wondered if he had forced her into a corner, if she was just thinking of marrying that guy to escape Sam Grayson and his damned overpowering desire, and if that was true he had to let her know that it wasn't necessary. He would put a lock and chain on his hands, he'd place himself under a twenty-four-hour guard, before he'd make her flee in such a manner.

She managed a small smile of her own, but she didn't say that she wouldn't go.

"Tell the kids I'll see them tomorrow," Rachel said, turning her back to him.

"No."

She whirled, faced him. "You don't want me to come back? You think it's best to end it now?"

He thought it was best to never end it. It would have been best for him if he'd kept her buried in his memories. But she was here; he'd sought her out. Now it was only his fault if he was in danger of burning up and dissolving into cinders.

He shook his head. "Tomorrow's the Tucker Summerfest. We close the yard. Remember? I'll be taking the kids. That's what I wanted to tell you."

Never mind that he had planned on asking her to come with them. It was obvious she needed some personal space.

He needed her to know that he could keep his distance, that if she stayed it would be okay.

"I want you to take the day off, have a day just for you. Maybe we'll see you there," he said.

He could tell by the stillness of her expression that it wasn't likely to happen. He had given her a reprieve. She had taken it.

"Maybe," she said. That was all.

And maybe in no time at all, she would be Mrs. Don Bowers. He would have lost Rachel Allyn for the second time in his life.

Chapter Nine

Rachel looked in the mirror, adjusted the delicate gold chain she'd looped around her neck.

Sam Grayson didn't pity Michelle Wilkins. The words swirled into Rachel's consciousness, blurring the picture in the mirror.

He wanted to help that little girl—because her clothes were ragged and her father drank away the grocery money.

But he didn't pity her. The enormity of what Sam had revealed yesterday swelled inside Rachel's soul as she stood before the mirror trying to decide what she would wear to the Summerfest.

Catching up a pair of white denim jeans and a red midriff top, Rachel sat down on the bed and pulled on the pants. Not that it mattered in the long run what Sam had or hadn't felt years ago. That didn't change things. He had still loved and married Donna. He was still not going to love Rachel Allyn.

But although she had regrets for all the years of friendship she had missed with Sam, she also could feel good knowing she hadn't been wrong about him when she'd first met him. Sam *was* an admirable man, he was a wonderful man, and he respected her, liked her, even if it would never amount to more than that. Someday, maybe, when she'd learned not to let Sam make her senses spin, maybe the two of them really could be friends.

Someday. A long time from now.

Still, someday was better than never.

With great determination Rachel pulled the red top over her head and tried out a tremulous smile, checking the mirror to see if it worked. "Let's go," she said, taking a deep, energizing breath. "It's party time."

She'd been wandering around, chatting to old friends, admiring the beautiful day and nibbling on hot dogs, when she felt Annie come up behind her. The little girl slipped her hand inside Rachel's palm as if it was the most natural thing in the world to do.

"Rachel," she said, shaking her head. "We are late. Zach tumbled into the mud, Daddy had to give him a new bath, and then Janey lost Baby. We are late, late, late. Is it almost over?"

"No, silly, of course not." Rachel brushed the little girl's nose with the tip of one finger. She noticed that Sam didn't come near with Janey and Zach.

"What should we do?" Annie asked, as if there was no question that they would be sharing this day together.

"An-nie," Sam drawled, moving closer then. "This is Rachel's day off. She probably has friends she hasn't seen for quite a while. Come on, pumpkin, we'll go check out the rides and see the pet display."

"Woof," Zach said in agreement.

But Annie was clearly not happy with Sam's statement, and Rachel found that she had to agree with the little girl. If she had so little time left, she wanted to live it to the fullest, saturate herself with Grayson family memories, fill herself to the top with visions of Sam and his children.

Rachel knew she had to end things, for she could never hurt the children, and she couldn't be a martyr, even for love. But that didn't mean the end had to be right now, this second. She had time. Even Don wouldn't be here until tomorrow and even then—even then—

"Hey, Zach, what do you say? Let's go take a whirl on the merry-go-round and find those woofs, huh?"

Rachel smiled into the little boy's eyes—and found that Sam had been caught in her line of vision. He was standing there, holding two babies, his legs splayed, his blue eyes still clear, if unreadable, beneath the shadow of his Stetson.

"I don't know about this," he said. "I thought we agreed—"

"I don't remember any agreement," Rachel said softly. "At least not one concerning this day."

Still he stood, a wall, a statue, a man who was determined to do what he considered to be the right thing—just the way he always had.

"It's just one day, Sam," she reminded him. *Not forever.* "Besides, I understand you've already had your hands full today. You were detained, late."

His smile slowly formed; it reached his eyes as he nodded his head to Janey, who was bucking in his arms.

"They're a little overexcited," he admitted.

So was she.

Rachel nodded. "Everybody's excited when a festival comes to town. Come on, Annie, let's go see what there is to see."

And see everything they did. She and Sam each took a twin. They sandwiched Annie between them and rode up and down on prancing painted stallions. They chased each other on the helicopters. At the pet display they watched the judges try to decide which chicken had the most personality.

Janey clapped her hands when the judge handed out the blue ribbons. Zach tried to climb down from Sam's grasp to get a closer look at the "woofs." Together they looked at chickens and cats, dogs and rats, gerbils and fish, oohing and aahing and pointing until the twins got tired and Sam settled with them on a bench in the corner.

Annie and Rachel moved on. They were looking at a pretty little golden retriever when Annie poked her fingers at the wire cage.

"I'd like to have a dog someday. Mommy didn't like pets."

Rachel knelt down to Annie's level. She prayed for the right words, the ones that would make a difference "I seem to recall that your mother was allergic to dogs," she answered truthfully.

Annie nodded. "That's what Daddy said, but Mommy said they were pests to take care of. Rachel?"

"Yes, Annie." Rachel let the little dog lick her finger, his rough tongue curling around her skin.

"Do you think my mommy might ever come for a visit?"

Rachel froze for two whole seconds. She forced herself not to close her eyes, to breathe normally, as she turned to the child. "I don't know, Annie," she finally admitted, pulling the little girl close for a hug. "I'm sorry, but I don't know that."

"Nicky says that you might get married soon, that you might go."

It was a loaded statement. Rachel did hold her breath then. She studied the angles of the comment that was really a question.

"I don't know if I'll be getting married anytime soon, Annie, but you realize I'm an employee. That means I just work for your dad. I can't stay with you forever."

Annie was biting her lip; she clenched her little hands. "I know. That's what Mrs. Nelson was, but—"

"But," Rachel continued, soothing her hand over the child's hair. "Even though I can't stay with you for always, Annie, I won't ever really leave you. I'm exceptionally loyal to my friends. We'd see each other sometimes, I'd talk to you on the phone, and hey, I write a really mean letter. Ask your aunt Kate. We've been long-distance friends for years, and you—you'd write a pretty great letter yourself. After all, you're Annie Grayson, the born storyteller."

Silence. So much painful silence.

"When will you go?"

"I don't know. Soon. But Annie, I *will* tell you. I won't surprise you. I would never simply slip away... I won't do that. I won't vanish. That's a promise."

Annie hugged her arms around Rachel's legs suddenly. She hid her face against Rachel.

"And you would call me? You'd write?"

Rachel closed her eyes; she smoothed Annie's silky hair. "The phone cords will be burning up, Annie. I swear it."

With that the little girl pulled back. She stared all the way up into Rachel's eyes as a tear slipped down her cheek and trembled on her chin. "Then make them short phone cords, Rachel, please. I don't like long ones. I don't."

Neither did she, Rachel wanted to say. But it would only make things harder for Annie if she allowed the child to see just how little she wanted to leave.

Instead, she nudged one finger under the little girl's chin, brushing the teardrop away. She smoothed two fingers across Annie's damp cheek. "I meant what I said, Annie," she whispered. "I don't turn my back on my friends. I stay in touch. And I hope...maybe you'll send me some of your stories. I'd love to see them."

Annie nodded, slowly, sadly, her expression too wise for for her years. "I will. I promise. And I'll water your flowers, too, Rachel. I like those flowers."

Rachel's throat felt tight and twisted. "Me, too, but not as much as I like *you,* Annie. I'm very glad I had the chance to meet you." She opened her mouth to say more, but she'd said all it was possible to say without offering hope where there was none, without making the damage worse.

Instead she simply continued to stroke Annie's hair. She looked up across the display area and into Sam's eyes. He had hired her to help Annie. Now he watched as she proceeded to hurt his child, the one she had promised to protect.

The afternoon had passed into evening. Annie had been persuaded away from Rachel by Nicky and Michelle. Hal and his friend Lily Dawson had asked if they could have the twins for a few hours. And when the dance floor had been set up and the music started, Rachel had managed to keep a crowd of humanity between her and Sam.

Slow music. Sensual music. Skin-to-skin music.

Looking up, Rachel spotted Sam in a millisecond. He was threading his way through the crowd, headed her way.

Taller than most men, his progress was easy to follow. Not that height alone made Sam stand out from a crowd. That slightly long, dark hair; the touch of swagger that emphasized his lean hips; and those blue, blue eyes, all were parts of Sam that set him apart.

Rachel knew she should probably go home right now, call it a day, anything to keep her distance from this man and to stop herself from doing what she was wanting to do.

Instead she stepped out onto the dance floor beneath the stars. She looked up at Sam when he made it to her side.

"I'll take that dance you owe me now, Rachel," he said, holding out his hand.

She placed her fingers in his, nodded. "This time I'll stay until the song's over, Sam."

It was just a dance. Lots of people were dancing.

Bracing her senses for the touch that had sent her spinning so long ago, she took a deep breath. Sam's hand against her back was just a part of the dance, nothing special, just a formality. But when Sam gave a tug and pulled her closer into his arms, Rachel knew there was nothing formal about the way she was feeling.

Leaning her head on his shoulder, Rachel moved with him. As Sam turned and swirled her, as he waltzed her around the makeshift wooden floor, she closed her eyes.

"Tired?"

She looked up and found only the star-spangled night, only Sam, as she leaned back against the flesh and steel of his arm. "Not at all."

He smiled then, brushing his hand over her hair, pulling her back to her resting place against his chest.

This was where she felt at home, this was where she'd once wanted to be.

This was the man she loved. Had always, would always love. The thought plunged in, as unavoidable as a red light in a darkening sky. No matter who or what came or went in her life, there would always be Sam waiting in her thoughts, slipping into her dreams. It was the truth. She knew that, but the truth caught her unprepared. Rachel stumbled slightly.

Sam lifted her off her feet, holding her close till she could get her bearings, then pulled her in tight against his hips as he waltzed her back into the dance.

Rachel locked her hands around Sam's neck, holding on, connecting herself to him. She drank in the warm male scent of him: soap, a touch of lime-scented after-shave. If she turned her lips a fraction of an inch, she'd be kissing the muscles of his chest.

And if things had been different years ago, if she'd been older, if she hadn't pushed Sam's friendship away, if there'd been no Donna for him to love, maybe this wouldn't be the first dance ever she was sharing with Sam. Maybe it wouldn't be the last.

But she was not going to dwell on that now. Not yet. For a few minutes more, he was hers. All hers.

Rachel smiled against Sam's shirt, and he tucked her closer to his heart.

"I never knew you danced so well, Sam," she murmured.

He moved slightly, his lips catching on her hair. "And whose fault would that be, I wonder?"

"Mine, Sam. All mine." She took the blame; she took the man to her heart.

He shook his head. "Mine, too, I think. You wouldn't have walked away without a reason."

He was right, but she didn't want to waste time explaining now. Rachel gave herself up to the dance—and Sam.

Sam spread his hand wide across Rachel's back. He could feel the warmth, imagine the softness beneath the thin material of her blouse. Her hair swayed as she moved, brushing against his fingers. He wanted to wrap it around his wrist, breathe in the lemony scent of it. He wanted to tilt her head back so that her long mane draped down her spine and her creamy white neck was exposed to his lips.

But he did none of those things. Instead he held her, just a little too close. He let his thoughts drift into territory that was just a touch too dangerous. Hell, who was he trying to kid? His thoughts were way *too* dangerous. He'd allowed himself to imagine holding Rachel in his arms for more than just this moment, of keeping her against his heart through long days and even longer nights.

Sam shifted, dodging his errant daydreams. He forced himself to smile reassuringly down at Rachel when she looked up at him. What would she say if she knew what he'd been thinking?

He didn't want to know.

Hard to believe he was holding her at all. She'd made a living out of keeping him a room's length away.

But what if she hadn't? What if he hadn't chased her away with words he now knew he'd uttered but couldn't remember? Would she have continued to smile at him? Would he have felt the way he was feeling now? Would he have married a woman who had been too young to commit to a relationship?

Sam closed his eyes. He didn't know the answers to any of those questions. Instead, he just held on. He tightened his grip on Rachel and she looked up at him. She sank back into his embrace, becoming a part of him, making him a part of her.

He wanted this woman like a drowning man wants an island in the ocean. But he couldn't have her—and he didn't blame her. Not at all.

She'd restored his trust, that deep-in-the-soul faith in a person that he thought he'd never know again. Because he knew that she would never betray a man without a reason. She would never wound or abandon a child if she could help it.

He believed in her. Implicitly. He would trust her to supply the very air that he breathed—but there was no point in thinking that way. Because he'd learned his lesson. Sam Grayson would never again push a woman into a commitment she wasn't ready for. He wouldn't unintentionally harm Rachel again.

Besides, although he might want, he might trust, he might feel passion that threatened to melt his soul—it was no more than that. This thing he felt for Rachel wasn't more than that. It couldn't be.

The music dipped and Sam slid his hand lower on Rachel's back. His fingers touched the soft curve of her hip as he braced her for the turn. A slight shiver ran through her slender frame, and Sam felt her quiver against him.

"Cold?" he asked. "I could find you a sweater." But he made no move to step away from her.

And she made no move to leave the circle of his arms. "Sam," she said softly, "I'm no hothouse flower." Her lips moved against his shoulder, and he knew that she was smiling.

He pulled back, just to see that sweet smile that turned her eyes to stars. For long seconds she looked up, watching him, sharing the sunlight and moonlight and magic that was a part of her.

Marry me. The words filled his mind and his heart, and he knew that he couldn't deny the truth any longer. Like it or not, he loved this woman. She was his heart, his all. He would go to hell and back a million times just for her.

Marry me.

Sam opened his mouth, then closed it again. He was not going to ask. He was not going to do something so foolish as to ask.

"Marry me, Rachel," he whispered, letting the music drift past him, slowing their steps to a halt as he watched her...and waited. "Come stay with us. Come live in my house."

For one brief moment, time moved in slow motion. Rachel leaned into him, her fingers tightened around his neck, he could swear those lovely lips were lifted for a kiss.

He almost thought he saw "yes" in her eyes.

And then, she stopped, frozen in place. His hands at her waist, Sam could feel her inhaling a long, deep breath. She stiffened, bit her lip. He knew the second the light fled her face. Still staring at him, she looked at him through eyes filled with want and need—and denial.

"Sam," she said, her voice a low moan as she slipped her hands away from his shoulders and down to his forearms as if she meant to push him away. But she didn't.

"I—oh, Sam," she repeated sadly, leaning back against his still-locked arms as she shook her head.

"I—I'm sorry, Sam. About this—about Annie. Especially Annie. But I don't think—" She bit her lip, shook her head again.

And her eyes that had been shining such a short time ago, began to mist over. Sam closed his eyes. Coward that he was, he couldn't bear to think that he'd made her cry.

Silently he damned himself for even asking the question. It had clearly been a mistake. She had not wanted or expected this, and hadn't he, only short moments ago, promised he wouldn't push her? Hell, what a liar he was. He'd pushed her, tried to manipulate her, since the moment he'd stepped back into this town. He'd gotten into her face, into her space, he'd used her warm heart and her giving ways to get what he wanted from her. She had told him that she hadn't met the right man, and yet here he was trying to bully her into feeling something for him. He was hurting her, and it was damn well going to stop now, no matter how much pain he had to go through himself.

As if from a distance, he heard the music stop, felt the shuffle of feet as people left the dance floor, yet he still stood there, trying to find his voice, to let Rachel know that he hadn't intended to cause her distress. He heard the rising murmurs of the crowd, the footsteps that came closer, yet his eyes were locked with the lady's, and neither of them seemed able to break away.

"Rachel!" The voice came from close by. An unfamiliar, male voice. Cries of "Hey, Don," fell on Sam's back.

Opening his eyes, he tensed, stepped closer to Rachel, turned so that his back was to the voice. "Rachel?" he coaxed, sliding his hands up her back.

Her anguished eyes widened, she shook her head again, ignoring the sounds emerging behind them. Rising on her toes, she lightly brushed his lips with her own, but Sam could feel goodbye in her kiss. "I can't marry you, Sam," she whispered. "I wish I could."

"There you are, Rachel. Sweetheart, are you hard to find," the deep male voice swept in, crushing the rest of her words.

Sam felt a slight tap on his shoulder. He turned toward the man whose attention was all on Rachel and looked into a smiling, congenial face. The man was handsome, sandy-haired and green-eyed, nearly as tall as Sam. He was nodding, holding out his hand to Rachel as if he clearly expected her to go with him.

"Rachel, angel, I've been looking all over for you." The man's voice was filled with genuine warmth, his soft drawl was tinged with caring. "I couldn't wait that extra day, not another twenty-four hours, had to see you now. Come with me?" he asked. "Honey, it's been forever."

And when Rachel looked up, stared into the man's eyes, Sam saw the man's glow of welcome. It was clear that the legendary Don Bowers loved this lady to distraction. And

Sam recognized that *he* was the intruder here, the new kid on the block.

Carefully he released Rachel, gave her a curt nod of thanks for the dance and faded back into the crowd.

He walked away from the lady and closed his mind to the thoughts that threatened to make him turn and snatch her back.

Once again he had lost Rachel Allyn. The only difference was this time he knew what he'd lost. He knew at last that this feeling couldn't die, it couldn't be killed, it wouldn't dissipate with time. For what he felt for Rachel was love. Definitely love, and he was scared as hell that it was the forever kind.

As he plunged into the crowd, located his children and rounded them up for the trip home, Annie tugged on his hand.

"Could we ask Rachel to come home with us tonight, Daddy? I want to tell her about all the things I did today."

Sam looked down at the eager face turned up to his. Slowly he shook his head. "We can't expect Rachel to come running whenever we want her to, pumpkin. She has her own life."

"I know, Daddy. We talked. We did. I know Rachel's an—umployee, but I thought maybe tonight...just this night..." Her eyes were wide, her voice soft and pleading.

Sam knelt down, he ran a hand over his daughter's soft curls, took her hand in his. "I'm sorry, not tonight, Annie. Rachel won't be coming tonight."

And maybe not any other night, Sam thought, as he headed his children toward home. But he needn't make Annie face that fact just yet. He'd take the pain alone tonight. One grieving Grayson was enough for now.

Rachel felt suddenly cold when Sam let go of her. She whirled, looking for him, but he'd already turned his back.

He was walking away without a backward glance.

And Don was standing beside her, smiling like a big, overeager puppy.

For a moment Rachel just stood there, swaying on her feet.

Sam had asked her to marry him. She had turned him down. She wanted to run away, to lick her wounds, to hide from the fact that Sam had seen her talking to Annie earlier and had done what he'd felt was necessary to secure his child's happiness. Hadn't he said that he would do anything, absolutely anything for his children? Did that include steeling himself to marry a woman, when he'd already decided that marriage was not for him?

Rachel couldn't face that question and the inevitable answer. She'd grown up witnessing her own mother's pain at being married to a man who didn't love her. She knew that there was no happiness for anyone in that direction. And yet how could she deal with the fact that she had thrown away the chance to stay with Sam and his family forever? She couldn't. Instead, she looked at Don who was chatting quietly beside her. Don had been a patient man, he had waited for her a year. He deserved better than she was giving him this moment. He deserved her full attention.

Taking a deep breath, she managed to turn. She even managed to smile.

"Nice try, angel," he said, leaning forward and brushing her forehead with his lips. "But if that isn't the most pathetic smile I've ever seen, then I'm sadly in need of glasses. Want to tell good old Don all about it?"

The way he said "good old Don" made fresh tears start to build deep within Rachel. Don was such a kind man, such a wonderful man.

He was everything a woman should want in a man, but he didn't have a low, caressing Texas drawl that stroked her senses with every word; he didn't have eyes that reminded a woman of a bottomless, warm Caribbean sea; he didn't make her feel that she would dry up and blow away if she couldn't have him; he didn't have three children that she loved beyond all belief. Don was a man any woman would be proud to love and yet . . .

"Oh, Don," she said, looking up into his eyes and struggling to find her voice. "I'm so sorry," she said, her voice thick with unshed tears.

"Uh-uh," he whispered, linking her arm through his and starting to walk. "That's not what I came to hear. There's no way that I'm going to listen to that kind of talk."

"But I should have called you before. I shouldn't have waited for you to come and find me like this. You've been so patient, so caring, and I thought I might—I wanted so badly to give that back to you, but . . ."

The pressure of his fingers on her arm increased slightly, then let up. "You never made me any promises, Rachel. You told me last summer that you didn't care enough. I'm an adult. I took the chance, I knew the risks." His voice was forgiving, but weary. He swiped a hand over his jaw.

"So how long have you known that you loved this guy?" he asked suddenly.

Rachel stopped in her tracks.

"It shows?"

He shrugged, continued walking, slipping her hand down to rest in his. "Let's just say that I study you a little closer than the average human being, Rachel. Your secret's probably safe with me."

She smiled at him then, a watery but genuine smile. This man was so special, so dear.

"If it's any consolation, Don, I wish it was you that I was in love with. And I want—that is, I'm hoping that we still can be friends."

At that he stopped walking. He turned to her, face-to-face, and slowly shook his head. "You'd be a good friend, Rachel, but what I feel for you isn't friendship. No man who loved you could ever settle for just being friends—so, no. Much as I'd like to please you and make you happy, no. That's something I can't do. At least not now while the feeling's so strong. You understand?" he said gently, his voice strained, his hands just a shade too tight on her own.

Did she understand? How could she not, when she was remembering that only a short while ago Sam had suggested that they remain friends. That was what he wanted to offer her: friendship, desire, marriage, children. Everything, in fact, that she wanted—except love.

And like Don she knew now that friendship would never work between her and Sam. Sooner or later she'd slip. Sooner or later she'd cry. And Sam would see.

"I understand," she agreed.

Don nodded. He lifted his hand and gestured toward the other side of the slowly clearing festival grounds. "You'd better go if you want to catch that guy. Looks like this place is clearing out. I didn't mean to interrupt your conversation. I was just hoping—well, you know what I was hoping." He shrugged, pulled his hand from hers and shoved it in his pocket. "Well, you'd better leave now. And, Rachel?"

She looked him straight in the eye. He deserved so much, but this was the best she could do.

"I appreciate your honesty, honey. You didn't try to lie to me. Ever. You didn't hide from the truth."

Don's words followed her as she walked away and went in search of Sam and Annie. He was wrong, so wrong. She'd spent a lifetime hiding from the truth. At fifteen she had hidden herself from Sam, never explaining to him why she had turned away from their friendship. If she had done that, if she had confessed, well—it wouldn't have changed things for her, but maybe Sam would have been happier. She had hurt him by her silence, she knew that now. She wouldn't do that again. He had been ripped apart by his divorce, scorned by a woman he'd loved. And while Rachel knew this was the end of things for her and Sam, she could not leave him thinking that she had rejected him, too.

Even if it cost her more pain than she could ever recover from, this time she would not sacrifice Sam's ego for her own. He would know that her reason for turning him down was not that she didn't want him, but that she wanted him too much to settle for less than his love.

She would make arrangements to see the children from time to time on their own, if Sam would allow it. She would tell him the truth, that only a fool who loved him would have said no to his marriage proposal, and then—well, she'd think about what happened next later.

There was only one thing that Rachel was sure of at this moment. She knew that there was only one man she had ever loved and ever would love. If there was to be no Sam in her future, there would be no wedding bells, either.

If she could not have Sam's love, then Hal and Lily would never dance at her wedding.

Chapter Ten

At home Sam tossed and turned in the big queen-size bed, a bed that was way too big for a man who was going to spend the rest of his life sleeping alone.

The scrawny feather pillow lying beside him was a poor substitute for the woman he loved. It lay there, immobile, lumpy and cold. Swearing, he sat up in bed, scrunched the pillows behind him, staring out the darkened window.

This place was her, through and through, Sam thought, and he realized for the first time that he hadn't bought this house with only Annie in mind. From the first moment he'd seen Rachel Allyn bent over that file cabinet, she'd filled his thoughts, she'd nourished his soul, he'd wanted her near him, around him. He'd wanted to please her. And those sweet-smelling roses Rachel had nurtured, the ones whose scent drifted through his window and filled his garden, were going to haunt him forever. He wanted them to haunt him, he wasn't going to get rid of them just to make it easy to forget.

Sam leaned closer to the window, drinking in the rose-filled night, but the soft ring of the bedside phone cut his thoughts in two. Frowning, he reached for it.

"Sam?" Rachel's voice broke the night when he finally managed to find the receiver in the dark. "We need to talk."

Like hell they would talk. He knew what she was going to say. She'd just come from her meeting with Don Bowers, maybe she was with him still. Sam sucked in a breath, forcing himself not to think about Rachel cuddled up to that green-eyed, handsome man.

He sighed, knowing this moment was unavoidable. Somehow, sometime, she was going to walk down the aisle with a man who wasn't Sam Grayson. Sooner or later he'd have to wake up to that fact. "All right, we have to talk," he agreed. "But the kids are in bed. I can't leave them alone."

"No. No, of course you can't." Her voice whispered over his bare skin. "Did you think I'd ask that? I'll be there, Sam. Soon."

Too soon. Much too soon. He ached for her, and yet he didn't want her here at night, in the shadows, in the darkness that would tempt him to touch her. He wanted the blazing, brain-numbing, eye-opening sunlight full in his face. He wanted a glare that would blind him to all the sweet and lovely things that she was. But he could see her point in making this a night visit. If she was tendering her resignation, she wouldn't want the children to have to hear—and neither would he.

"I'll leave the porch light on," he agreed, hanging up and reaching for his jeans.

Ten minutes later he stood there in the yellow glow of the outside light, watching her pull up in that cute little red car of hers.

She climbed out, still wearing that red-and-white number she'd had on earlier today, the one that did mean and terrible things to his sanity. Sam focused his attention on her face, but that was no better. He'd always been a sucker for great gray eyes and kiss-me-now-please lips, at least when they were Rachel's eyes and Rachel's lips.

Unable to stand there and watch her walk to him, he met her halfway, outside the perimeter of the light.

"I want you to know that I'm sorry for everything I conned you into, Rachel," he began, his voice rough and gravelly. "You'll be wanting to go now. I've heard all about Don Bowers, and it's ten kinds of obvious that he's a great guy, who's absolutely in love with you."

Rachel raised her chin, she looked directly into his eyes. Sam wanted to groan. He shoved his hands deeper into his pockets.

"Yes," she agreed. "Don's a very nice man."

"Then you'll be marrying him," he said. "I expect that's true, and you don't have to worry about the kids. I've heard that Cynthia Watts's niece is looking for a job. I understand that you'll want to be leaving right away, that Don has job-related commitments he'll need to get back to."

He couldn't believe he was saying this, that he was talking to her as if they were discussing the week's grocery list.

Rachel looked into Sam's eyes, but the darkness hid his expression from her. His voice, however, was as clipped and cold as Alaska in winter. He couldn't be making his point more clear. If she had ever harbored any doubts about the fact that Sam didn't love her the way a man loved a woman, they were dying. She *was* dying, but she couldn't give in to her grief right now. She had promised herself that she was done with hiding from the truth. She wanted to be honest with Sam.

But his words, his generosity in stepping away in an attempt to make things easier for her, cut deeper than she had imagined she could be cut.

"Would you stop being so darn nice to me, Sam? Would you just once, please, not make me feel like you're trying to help me? Wasn't that what you told Donna years ago, what I heard you say, that I was poor and poverty-stricken and that I needed your help?"

The words sounded childish i Rachel's ears. They sounded just the same way they had many years ago.

Instantly Sam's expression melted. He drew her back into the light, he placed his arms about her, warming her with his body. "*Did* I say that, sweetheart? If I did, I didn't mean it to hurt you. I only meant that I *wanted* to help you. I'll always want to help you."

"Sam..." Rachel's voice came out low and nearly incomprehensible. "That's not what I want from you."

She felt him freeze, felt his lips on her hair. "What *do* you want from me, darlin'? You want me to let you go? You want me to let you marry that guy? I'm doing it. Hell, I'm doing it, aren't I?"

Rachel couldn't have stopped herself from twining her arms around Sam's waist if an army of police officers had ordered her not to. He was here, he was warm and safe, and he was kissing her, holding her. And they were alone...

"I'm not marrying Don," she said, her voice muffled against his chest.

She felt strong fingers gently close around her chin, she tipped her head up to meet Sam's gaze.

"You still haven't met the man you could love, then?" he asked, sliding his thumb along her jawline.

Long seconds ticked by. She took a deep breath, but she didn't drag her gaze from his own.

"I never said that," she said quietly.

"That's a lie, Rachel Allyn." Sam's words were hard, but his voice was whisper soft.

She shook her head slowly, her skin sliding against his fingers.

"I said I'd never met the right man, one I could love and who would love me back," she offered.

Sam closed his eyes, she felt a shudder run through him. When he opened his eyes again, there was a dangerous glint in those deep blue depths. He tilted his head and lightly brushed her dry lips.

She swallowed hard.

"You turned me down when I asked you to marry me today, darlin'," he said carefully. "Would that be because you don't love me?"

Rachel thought she would never find her voice. She wasn't sure she wanted to find her voice ever. Sam was staring at her, holding her in place simply by looking at her. She'd promised to offer him the truth, she wanted to simply answer his question, but the naked truth was so damning.

She took a deep breath, her effort bringing her breasts up against Sam's chest. Licking her lips, she let out a sigh.

"I saw you watching me with Annie today," she finally said. "Sam, I *know* how much your children's happiness means to you. I *know* how it must have made you feel to see her hurt. You'd do anything for those babies. I would, too. I'd do almost anything, except—marry a man who didn't love me."

"You think I don't love you?" Sam stepped forward, lightly nudging Rachel back. She found herself against a porch post, sandwiched between Sam's hard body and a solid piece of wood. His legs straddled hers, but she wouldn't back down. She tilted her head higher and stared at him dead-on.

"I think you love your child so much that you'd sacrifice everything for her, and I'm not blaming you for it, but Sam, I've been there. Two fathers, neither of whom seemed to love my mother. I swear I don't know how she survived it, because she sure as death loved them. I don't even know how I came out of the whole thing intact, except for the fact that she practically loved me to pieces and I had this whole family of babies who loved me back just as hard. But I was a child, Sam. I wasn't a woman loving a man who didn't really want me."

"And you think I'm that same kind of man?"

When she nodded, Sam swore, an ugly word that he'd surely never use in the bright light of day. He took a step back, and Rachel felt as if her bones had turned to butter, as if the only thing that was holding her up was the hard wooden pole behind her back. But she managed to put her hand up, to place her fingers over his lips to keep him from swearing again.

"I didn't mean that as an insult, Sam. A man who cares so much about a child—how could I be offended by that? I think you're a wonderful man, a kind man, a good man."

"A very nice man?" he asked, repeating the words she'd used to describe Don.

With his gaze turned from hers the words flowed easier. Rachel even managed a smile at his offended tone. "More than a very nice man, Sam. I came here tonight to explain to you what you once said you wanted me to explain. The reason I ran away from you for so long, the reason I hid myself from you was because I was afraid that you pitied me. And—" She pressed harder on his lips when he started to shake his head and speak. "I know now that wasn't true. I know you were just being Sam, just trying to help someone who needed it. But it wasn't your help I wanted, Sam. That was never what I wanted."

She turned her own head away when his gaze locked on hers.

He didn't ask what she wanted. By now he must know, but she licked her lips, she made herself go on. "I've loved you all of my life, Sam, even when I was just a kid. I didn't want you to know, to see. I've hidden it from you, maybe even from myself, but it's always been there. I've always cared. That's why I can't marry you. I wanted you to know that it wasn't you that was the problem. It's me."

Sam slid his hands against her cheeks, threaded them through her hair. "You think it's a problem that you love me?" he asked, his voice thick and rough. "And what if I told you that I loved you back?"

Her breathing stopped, her body gave an involuntary jerk. She forced herself to remember just how Sam had looked when he'd seen Annie hurting today. She tried not to remember the look in the child's eyes herself.

"Sam," she said, through the tears that were rising in her throat. "Annie wouldn't be happy if she knew that things weren't right between us."

"You don't believe that I love you?" Sam asked, dropping a kiss on her ear.

Rachel breathed in quickly, trying to ignore the sensitive nerve endings that Sam's kisses were affecting.

She clutched the front placket on his shirt, asking him to look at her. "You—you told me that you'd never want love or marriage again...but I wouldn't blame you, Sam, for wanting to marry a woman you thought would be a good mother for Janey and Zach and Annie. I just—"

"You just—don't want to be that woman, even if you do love me to distraction?" Sam asked, raising one lazy brow.

Sam was laughing at her. Rachel tipped her chin up a notch. She gave him the most disdainful frown she could muster, given the fact that she was still pressed tightly to his body. "I just want to know that I'm wanted for myself and not just for my way with a bowl of oatmeal, Sam," she said. "I'm not sure I can believe—that is, I've known you so long and you—you never loved me before."

Raking one hand up her arm, behind her neck, and cupping the back of her head in his palm, Sam studied her intently, as if he wanted to look right through her body and into her heart. "Does that mean you're still saying no, Rachel?"

She closed her eyes, blotting out those blue eyes that could convince her to do almost anything. "It means I don't know, Sam," she admitted. "I've said what I came to say and I—I'd like to go home now."

But when she started to open her eyes and step away, Sam didn't move. Instead he leaned over, took her lips with his own.

"Not this time, angel," he whispered. "This time you don't run. This time I'm not giving you the chance to slip away from me."

Gently he guided her to the porch swing, eased her back into its depths.

"Wait here," he said, looking sternly at her. "Don't go. Don't get up. If you do, rest assured that I'll come after you. I'm not standing by silently while you walk away from me again, Rachel."

"But where are you going?" she asked, as he pulled a pocketknife from his jeans and stepped off the porch into the darkness.

"I'm going to show you, Rachel," he said, his voice deep and low. "I'm going to woo you, to try to win you, I'm going to do all that I can to prove to you that I want nothing more than to wed you. But I've never been a man who knew the words, so..."

He disappeared into the night.

Concerned, she started to rise. The chain on the swing jangled.

"Stay, Rachel," she heard him say. "I don't want to have to wake the kids, but I will if I have to follow you. Please. Stay."

She stayed. She sat. She heard him rustling in the darkness, moving around the house. Once she heard him swear softly in the night. He was gone a long time, so long that she began to wonder why she had come. He'd said that he loved her. Sam had said that he cared, but it was so hard to believe. She'd loved him for so many years without being loved back....

And that was when she saw him, Sam standing just outside the circle of light, his body shadowed as he slid a single rose upon the edge of the porch.

"You were just a kid when we met," Sam said, placing another rose beside the first. "But you were sweet and warm and pretty."

He placed another rose next to the first two.

"I was dating Donna at the time, and...you were right before, when you said that she was very young. She was. So was I. We were all so young, so very, very young."

Another rose joined the first three.

"Sam?"

"Yes, love?"

Sam continued placing roses on the pile, one at a time. Slowly, very slowly.

"Sam, why are you doing this?"

He stopped then, for a second, looked up at her and smiled. "Because I ache for you, Rachel. I love you, and I want you to understand how deep that love goes, how much you mean to me. Even when you first came into my life, when you were still just reaching for adulthood, I always did find you absolutely enchanting. You fascinated me. I think

I must have loved you even when I thought you were too young. That's why I was so upset with Donna that day. I don't remember the words I said, but I definitely remember being angry with her, defending you. I never, *never* thought I would be the one to hurt you with my careless comment."

He placed another rose on the porch. And another.

"I wasn't hurt, Sam. I was—"

Sam slowed his movements. He stared at her across the space that separated them, and Rachel could swear she felt that gentle look touch her like a caress.

"Shh. I know what you must have felt, love. Don't defend me. I *did* hurt you, and I'll always be sorry for that. And when you retreated from me, I guess I let my ego stand in the way. I should have chased you, way back then. I should have waited for you to grow up. Instead, I licked my wounds in silence. I married a woman who was way too young herself, made her pay for my own mistakes. I did way too many things wrong, but . . . don't ever think that I don't care. I care, Rachel. I do."

Sam continued piling roses on the planks of the porch. Already there was a glorious scatter of loose, pink and red and white blossoms carpeting the floor.

Rachel rose to her feet. She ignored the forbidding look on Sam's face as he asked her to stay put and give him a chance to finish.

"I'm not a man who knows how to say the words, Rachel, but I'm trying. I *am* trying. You asked me if I was marrying you for my children. The answer is, I suppose, yes," he admitted. "How could it not be, when everything I do in this world impacts them? I want a woman who could love them, too. And I don't for one second believe you'd have it any other way."

His eyes were filled with tension now. Rachel knew it was hard for him to admit that he wanted her for the kids, when there was every chance that his words would damn him in her eyes. She took another step closer to the man.

He added a rose to the collection. She noticed he'd snagged one of his fingers with a thorn, and as she reached the edge of the porch, she dropped to her knees and took her hand in his. She cradled it to her cheek.

"I do love you, Sam," she whispered. "And I've made a few mistakes of my own."

She felt his hand jerk against her skin. "Rachel. Dammit, Rachel, you don't know how much I love you. So damn much. Do you think I'd really marry a woman just for my kids? Yes, I want them to have a good mother. I want them to have every blessed thing I could give them, but I wouldn't wed a woman I didn't love, heart and soul, not even for them. I know as well as you that would never work. I thought I'd never want to marry again. I tried to tell myself I'd never love again, but I didn't count on the woman I'd never really stopped loving in the first place. I didn't know that it was going to kill me to let you go. I'm not sure I could have done it when it came right to the moment of watching you walk out the door. I think I would have done everything in my power to stop you."

Rachel leaned forward then. She placed her arms around Sam's neck as he lifted her from the porch and held her to his heart. "I thought I would have to leave you, Sam. I didn't know how I could live here and never have your love. And," she said, pulling back and frowning at him, "I *never* wanted to be just friends," she admitted, letting her frown turn into a full-fledged smile.

Sam smiled back. He tilted her head and kissed the column of her neck. "Umm. What kind of a fool ever made that suggestion? Any idiot could see that I was totally incapable of being just friends with you. At least none of my friends I can think of would ever allow me to do this,'' he said, lifting his head and taking her mouth with his own.

''Then they don't know what they're missing,'' Rachel murmured, her lips sliding against Sam's. She ran her hands through his dark hair and brought her mouth back to his. ''I can't believe you plundered Annie's rose garden,'' she said when she finally pulled away and stared at the multitude of flowers blanketing the porch.

''You think my daughter would object to me doing everything I could to show you how much you mean to me? To us? I suspect that if she'd thought it would have worked, Annie would have been out here herself. She would have raided every garden in Tucker...and so would I,'' he admitted, lifting her off her feet and stepping up onto the porch with her in his arms.

Rachel rested her head against his shoulder. ''So you'd commit illegal acts for me, would you?''

She felt the low rumble of laughter roll through Sam's chest. ''That and more, Rachel. I never before fought for a woman's love or even wanted to. I certainly never stumbled around a dark rose garden fighting thorns before. But I would do much more than that, angel. I'll spend my life proving to you just how much I care. You're a different kind of woman, Rachel Allyn. My kind, and I'd do anything for you. Just you.''

''Just you, Sam,'' Rachel agreed, raising her lips to his own. ''It was always just you.''

The sun was just slipping up into the sky when Rachel looked up from her perch on Sam's lap. She wondered how his back was going to feel, pressed against the hard boards of the swing all night. The porch was a veritable garden of roses.

"Wow!" Annie's little voice rang out, and Rachel turned to see her coming out the door, flanked by two little sausage-shaped children in blue and pink sleepers.

"Wose," Janey said solemnly, reaching for one of the blossoms.

Rachel sat up higher, ready to pull the little girl away from the thorns, but Annie was already there, instructing her sister in the dangers of "biting" flowers. Rachel's sudden movement woke Sam, and he tightened his arms about her.

"Good morning, you little squirts," he said to his children in that sandy, sleepy voice of his.

Annie looked at the way Rachel was perched on her father's lap. She glanced down at the flowers scattered all over the place. Her eyes were wide, she chewed on her lip.

"What happened?" she asked hesitantly. "What are all the flowers for?"

Sam looked at Rachel, a question in his eyes. She smiled and took his hand, turning to Annie. "We're going to have a wedding, Annie. Would that be all right?"

"You're going to marry my daddy?"

The tentative question, the wary look about Annie, gave Rachel pause. Annie might not have wanted her to leave, but would she want to share Sam? Would she worry about Rachel taking her mother's place?

"We were thinking about it," Rachel said, ignoring the way Sam's hand clamped down on her own. She wondered if he was holding his breath the way *she* was.

Suddenly a smile broke through Annie's hesitance. She turned to Janey and Zach. "Rachel's staying," she announced with glee. "Rachel's going to live with us."

"Ra-chel," Zach said, totally proud of himself.

Janey simply tromped across the bed of flowers and held up her arms to be picked up.

"Woses," she repeated, when she was finally seated in the safe circle of Rachel and Sam's looped arms, and Annie and Zach had both climbed up on the swing, too.

"Yes, roses, sweetie," Rachel agreed. "What are we going to do with all these wonderful roses?"

Annie patted Rachel on the arm lightly. "We could put them in pots and take them to people, Rachel, couldn't we? We could share them. Flowers are for sharing," she said, repeating the words that Rachel had taught her.

Sam leaned down and kissed Rachel on the hair, on the cheek. "*Love* is for sharing," he added.

And Rachel couldn't have agreed with him more. As she leaned back into the arms of the man she loved, she knew that she had come home. Gathering her children close, she felt the warmth of Sam flowing through her as he tightened his arms about her.

Love had finally come out of hiding. Like a flower reaching for the sun, its partner in the dance of life, her heart turned toward the man who held her.

Rachel twisted in his embrace. With the twins now on her lap and Annie's hand clasped in her own, she lifted her lips for Sam's kiss. "You're right," she admitted. "So very right. Love—real love—can't hide in the dark. It's for sharing—for always."

"Share," Janey repeated, her voice a soft plea.

And Sam's laugh was low and sweet in Rachel's ears as they kissed their children, as they shared their love.

* * * * *

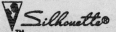

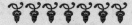

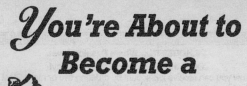